Debi Evans & *John MacPherson*

THE SECRET SOCIETY OF DRAGON PROTECTORS

'The City Guardians'

For Wicor Primary School

Debi Evans

Published by Debi Evans & John MacPherson

Cover design / illustration and chapter illustrations by John MacPherson

Published by Debi Evans & John MacPherson
Produced by Shore Books and Design, Blackborough End, Norfolk

ISBN 978-0-9554661-3-7

Books by

Debi Evans & John MacPherson

In

THE SECRET SOCIETY OF DRAGON PROTECTORS

Series

'The Dragon's Tale'

'The Cor Stan'

'A Shadow in Time'

'The City Guardians'

'The Silver Claw'

Contents

With special thanks to Jinty, Gus and Gran Mabel for all the love and support that has got me here; all my love John.

Chapter 1

'A Stormy Passage'

Full of fury, the rain came at them horizontally, resembling the piercing sword tips of an advancing army. For a moment Angus imagined he was back in the Middle Ages in the company of the knight George. He was not keen on violent storms and this one reminded him of the Trials in Krubera when they had to capture a bolt of lightning and he suddenly became acutely aware of the danger he was in. The dark clouds were suffocating as they closed in to envelope him. Bolts of lightning arced brightly and beautifully around them in a slow motion dance, allowing Pyrra to deftly glide around them as if perfectly in step with bass heavy music. Thunder boomed in Angus' ears but in a long drawn out manner that prolonged the rumble far longer than was natural. He thought of his parents sleeping in their bedroom in Kynton unaware of their son's peril. Then he remembered who his companion was and his concerns diminished as a feeling of calm and safety washed over him along with the relentless rain.

Angus forced his body forward and placed his right cheek against the wet but warm scales of Pyrra's neck. He closed his eyes listening to the reassuring beat of her wings and could feel the muscles in her back flex and strain as she worked strongly against the wind. Wispy tendrils of cloud caressed his face, condensing as it ran chilly over his skin. He reached up with his left arm he pulled his jackets heavy hood further over his face.

"How far have we come?" he called, half the sound being muffled by the hood that was shielding him from the elements.

"We're about half way I think..." she replied turning her head slowly to look at him. "Try to get some sleep" she added caringly.

Angus realised she was busy concentrating on the storm they had encountered and on maintaining her course to their destination so he settled his body as comfortably as he could in an attempt to do as she suggested.

The saddle he sat upon was not particularly comfortable and to be honest he did not need it to fly with Pyrra, but Mrs Tek had insisted on it for safety. Angus was as accomplished a flyer as Pyrra and they moved as one no matter what crazy maneuver she attempted. Whilst he lay with his eyes closed, Angus thought of what had happened in recent weeks. He recalled the theft of Dragonore from Krubera and the subsequent discovery of Felspar's plan to harm Ward Godroi; the unearthing of the portal, and traveling back in time to save the Ward. Not to mention the excitement of meeting the knight George and helping to scare off the invading Vikings. He thought about the knight's gift to him; the magnificent sword with which he slew Felspar, and finally, the fantastic news about Rhys's eggs.

The red dragon had laid the first dragon eggs for over a thousand years and their hatching was another event that signaled the end of the Great Hibernation. Dragons had decided to sleep away the Ages in order to avoid the relentless rise of Mankind which would have meant certain destruction of their species. Hibernation had kept all dragons safely hidden in everyday inanimate objects that had a dragon-like theme. They were to stay in this state of time-consuming slumber until the time was right for them to freely re-inhabit the earth, a time all dragons longed for. The Secret Society of Dragon Protectors, an organisation that Angus had helped re-establish, was now run by Rathlin Tek from his ancestral home. From the ancient seat Calmor Castle, situated on a remote island in the Irish

Sea, the Society carefully monitored all hidden dragons as they reawakened.

Angus was half dozing on Pyrra's back, his breathing matched hers so closely you could almost believe them to be one. He thought about the eggs and his imagination worked overtime, seeing the baby dragons hatch from the pearlescent shells that encased them. Unseen beneath his hood he smiled as he imagined them spouting flames from their tiny mouths and staggering in an ungainly fashion, like most newborn animals. Suddenly he had a strange thought so strong it forced him awake and Angus leaned forward to ask Pyrra a question.

"What do you call a baby dragon?"

The green dragon stayed silent and Angus felt compelled to repeat the question thinking his friend had not heard him above the raging storm. However, just as he thought about leaning forward again to shout louder she turned her head.

"Do you know, I can't remember!" exclaimed Pyrra with annoyance.

"Are you sure?" he asked again.

She shook her head to indicate she could not and Angus, never to be outdone by a challenge, probed further.

"Does it have anything to do with flames or sparks?"

"Sorry... they don't sound familiar" she replied turning her head away again.

Angus did not give up on this, and as they flew he suggested any and all of the names of baby animals he could think of; some of them like 'spawn' made Pyrra laugh.

"Cubs!" he shouted.

"Mmmm… that's not correct but it is on the right track" she looked deep in concentration, as if trying to solve an extremely difficult mathematical equation, "Wait a minute… whelps!" she shouted so suddenly that Angus almost slipped from his saddle.

"Whelps?" he replied. "What kind of word is that?" he asked.

"Fire Whelps to be exact!" she smiled. "I think it's Old English in origin but I don't know much more than that… perhaps you can look it up when we get back to Calmor" she replied turning her head towards him and looking very pleased she had remembered.

The Great Hibernation had taken its toll on her memory; a fact which irked her, and many other dragons enormously. Since her awakening by Angus she had gradually regained her memories. 'Still' she thought 'not bad for someone over two thousand years old!' Angus saw how pleased she was and

wondered what the young Fire Whelps would look like when they hatched. He grinned at the thought of taking one home to look after if Rhys ever needed a dragon sitter. He could just picture the look on his parent's faces as a young dragon accidentally set fire to the Kleenware boxes they stored in the garage that formed part of the Munro's home.

"How much longer to go?" he called to her, looking up sleepily.

"To our destination?"

"No, 'til the eggs hatch?" he asked.

"Oh about two weeks I should think"

Angus closed his eyes again as he snuggled in closer to Pyrra's scaly body and began to give in to sleep, lulled by the rhythmic beating of dragon wings.

The lad's mind wandered to his battle with Felspar, the black dragon they had finally defeated. Angus was glad that foul beast was no longer able to harm Rhys's babies or any other dragon for that matter, and he felt secure in the knowledge that Felspar was dead. It had been a titanic battle between the great knight George and the treacherous black dragon and as he slept through the raging storm, Angus began to think of that day. It was a dream he had replayed many times since the event and Angus could clearly see the knight as he strode into the middle of the village to face Felspar. George's shining helm and chain mail made a stark contrast to the black muscular body of the dragon and Angus watched as Pyrra used the knight's distraction to help the injured Godroi to safety. Soon the two combatants circled each other in what Angus thought was some sort of waltz of death, each looking for an opening to strike a killer blow. Then the battle suddenly started with blow after blow raining down on the knight, but he stood firm with his shield protecting him. The fiery breath of the dragon engulfed the knight and set fire to the buildings surrounding them. Even as Angus re-ran these memories he still felt concerned for George's life, such was the ferociousness of the onslaught. The knight had miraculously used his shield to protect himself from the flames and the countless blows from Felspar. As the dragon tired George began to parry and slash the beast with his sword, each blow cutting the black dragon with the precision of a surgeon. Angus watched closely as Felspar became angrier and angrier, until his rage took over and he lunged at George carelessly. This was the moment George thrust a killer blow into the hide of Felspar, a strike that had the black dragon writhing in agony and beaten.

Angus stirred slightly on Pyrra's back and

sensing his discomfort she turned her head towards him. She could not see his face but she heard him mumble in his sleep and she knew his mind was dealing with something very difficult. Replayed in Angus' mind, George strode forward to end the battle by issuing the final and fatal blow as Felspar lay helpless. Angus tensed up and wanted to cry out as the knight placed his shield on the ground. George raised his sword above his head, the point poised above the prone body of the black dragon, but in a flash Felspar slashed sideways. The black dragon rose up from the ground, delighted that his trick had worked. He strode towards the inert body of the knight as he lay on the ground next to the stone pillar his body had crashed into. Angus watched in horror as the whole scene replayed in his head like some horror movie he had seen many times. But before Felspar could kill the brave knight Pyrra appeared just in time to challenge the dark beast. Angus felt the same helplessness he did that day as Felspar taunted Pyrra before breaking the knight's sword, and that is when he grabbed the hilt. The weapon, normally too big and heavy for a lad of his size was easier to lift, but it still took all the strength he could muster to raise it from the ground. Angus ran at the beast, his anger forcing a dragon-like growl from his throat as he tried to run forward. He saw Felspar turn to face him and

Angus knew he needed to go faster. He needed the speed to allow the steel to penetrate the thick hide of the monster before him. As he had thought this, his body began to move faster than it had ever done without the benefit of Pyrra's dragon time. Angus had his eyes closed as the sword penetrated the flesh of the beast, shattering Felspar's Dragonore at the same time. He did not even see the retaliatory blow aimed by Felspar and by the time he came round Pyrra was asking him if he was okay.

Angus expected to wake up from this dream now as he had always done in the past, but instead he saw something else, something he had not seen before; Felspar staggering away from the scene of the battle. His heart pounded as he watched the dragon lurch towards the stream, and Angus expected to see the dragon fall there and die. As he observed, the black dragon stopped at the water, blood issuing from the rent in his chest. Angus waited expectantly for the dragon to succumb to the blue flames that would combust the beast from the inside out and leave nothing but ash and precious stones. Instead Felspar reached down and scraped the jewels from his injured chest and flung them into the stream. The black dragon then turned, painfully clutching his chest to stem the

blood flow and staggered towards the forest, and out of sight!

"Noooooo!"

Chapter 2

'Unusual Tourists'

"Angus, wake up!" shouted Pyrra, "What's wrong?"

"F… Felspar!" he stammered, "Alive!"

"What do you mean alive? He's dead Angus you've just had a bad dream" she soothed, "You were mumbling and shouting as you slept!"

"No Pyrra he's alive, I saw him brush the jewels into the stream and then limp off towards the forest!" replied the lad urgently.

"Think about it Angus. We both saw the terrible wound and the amount of blood. He is dead, you just had a nightmare… probably due to the storm" she smiled reassuringly.

Angus looked into her scaly face and despite her smile he noted the concern in her large green eyes.

"I guess you're right…" he conceded not wanting to distress her, "It just seemed so real"

Pyrra watched him for a second and then indicated forward.

"The storm's finished… and look…" she said.

Angus gazed past the green dragon's head and into the clear blue horizon. He could see a large landmass forming as Pyrra sped westwards using dragon time to shorten the length of the journey dramatically. In fact this particular power, that all dragons possessed, had allowed Pyrra to fly faster than a passenger plane; making the journey from the UK extremely fast indeed.

The area below grew in size as they drew nearer and Angus watched in fascination as more detail appeared. Soon, what looked like a vast island stretched out before them with a much larger landmass starting north of the island as it unfolded far behind. In fact it stretched so far that Angus could not make out where it stopped. It certainly looked like they had arrived in the United States and he wondered how much further it was to their particular destination.

"Not far now!" called Pyrra as if reading his mind.

The large island below them now became the focal point as Pyrra lined herself up with the coastline and followed it in a southwesterly direction. Angus was pleased the storm had passed and, pulling back his hood, he rubbed the sleep from his eyes. Feeling the chill wind slap his face and rejuvenate his senses, he was more confident that his nightmare was over. Of course Felspar was dead and it was stupid of him to doubt this.

His attention was drawn to passenger airplanes as they began to appear in the sky and Angus stared at the small windows in an attempt to see the people inside. They were too far away and fortunately for Pyrra she was moving too fast through and behind clouds for anyone to see her. Angus knew Flying in dragon time rendered a dragon visible while it concentrated power. This makes them most vulnerable to detection during this process, but with the benefit of enhanced speed they are usually too fast to be seen. The number of planes soon increased so much that Angus was concerned they would collide with one. He had been through that before and had no desire to experience freefall again. Now the island below became greyer as more and more buildings mushroomed out of the ground. Clearly they were nearing a large urbanised area and this was confirmed further as several airports came into view. Angus could now see that the large island looked connected to the larger landmass that had remained behind it from the point they had first seen it. He could also make out more and more details as they swept towards the point the terrain joined.

"Fasten your seatbelt as we are about to come in to land" called Pyrra in a cheery voice despite having just flown non-stop across the Atlantic Ocean.

The buildings below became larger and taller as

blocks of flats seemed to grow from the ground. The structures continued to get higher and higher until they congregated in the area Pyrra was aiming toward. Angus watched as the clouds cleared and below them was a sight he, like most people around the world, would recognise at once. He had seen most of these buildings and structures in many films and television programmes set in this famous city, and he felt a tinge of excitement as, one by one, they came into view. The lad fumbled in his backpack and retrieved a small book which Mrs Tek had given him before they left Calmor; a guidebook of New York City. He thumbed through the pages and much to the dragon's amusement, enlightened Pyrra on some of the more interesting facts about the world famous city.

The dragon, feeling mischievous, plunged forward almost causing Angus to lose the small guidebook. The East River sprung up so fast that he was sure they would hit the water, but just as he prepared to be soaked she pulled up, swooping under the famous Brooklyn Bridge with its grey stone towers standing proud like two soldiers on guard duty. She swept along the water passing under the riveted steel girders.

"HOLD ON!" bellowed Pyrra as the green dragon flew straight into the path of a large ferry coming the other way and then barrel rolled in an attempt to get out of the way!

Chapter 3

'Seeing Red'

Meredith Quinton-Jones, CEO of Quinton-Jones Drilling Limited was in a meeting in her office in Angel Street in the City of London. Her pale face and sharp features contrasted with her sleek and silky black hair. She wore an extremely expensive tailored suit in her favourite colour, which was red. Ms. Quinton-Jones' office was naturally lit by the winter sunlight, which flooded in from three large sash windows dominating the outside wall of the room. A large set of double doors broke up the opposite wall, stained in a deep mahogany red. The walls were covered half way with wooden panelling of the same colour as the doors and Meredith sat behind a large mahogany desk with her fingers clasped in front of her. Red was a very powerful colour, particularly when worn by this woman and it reflected in her surroundings. She was queen of this particular castle. At this moment she was considering how terribly vexed she was but through necessity she controlled her temper and met the current problem with as much patience as she could muster. The discussions within the office were very heated indeed, but this was not a difficult negotiation with

a client, or a board members meeting. The only other occupant of the room was one very angry dragon.

Felspar saw that Meredith had gone quiet and assuming she was about to give in he rose up to his full menacing height and cast a dark and foreboding shadow over the room as he spat with venom.

"I must go after them… this is my chance at revenge!" Meredith, un-intimidated by the black beast, drew in her breath and considered a decision she had made earlier in the day to begin a drilling operation in South East Asia. She had not been sure that it was the correct thing to do as the weather signs were not good for that region, but sometimes you had to take chances in business; something her father had taught her all too well. A growl brought her back to this current issue and placing her palms flat on the desk she slowly stood up, growing in stature herself as she raised her eyes to meet his. Felspar's eyes were flame red and furious but when he looked into Meredith's all he saw were pools of darkness; a cold calculating darkness that seemed to go on forever. Meredith smiled which only served to make her appear more intimidating.

"Now Felspar you know that makes no sense…" she answered addressing the dragon in a voice as businesslike as her surroundings, "We have a plan and we should stick to it!"

"But that was before I realised they would be so isolated!" replied the black dragon eagerly. "Don't you see we could be rid of them for good and then the SSDP could be ours? This is our chance! Once the others see their hero dead, believe me they will all crumble!"

"NO!" bellowed Meredith, her patience finally snapping as she slapped the palm of her hand on the desk. Then mustering herself-control, "You will do as I say" she hissed through gritted teeth. "The boy and the dragon can wait. They are no threat to us now and you will bide your time until I say otherwise." She waited for a response and satisfied that the argument was finally won she continued.

"I promise you Felspar, you will get your revenge… we both will, but now is not the time" she added smiling once more whilst stroking one of the spikes under the fearsome dragon's chin. "Besides I have another task for you… one that only you can be trusted with!"

"You mean this fool's errand you would have me complete? You insult me human!" he snarled.

"My dear Felspar I can assure you this is no fool's errand" she replied, "The artefact you will search for is the greatest of prizes and with it we will rule over all the dragons in the world, and no one will stop us. Not even our little friend!" she added, appeasing the angry dragon slightly.

She watched the glint in his fiery red eye as she stroked the side of his jaw. He turned his head to one side like a puppy and Meredith knew he had only capitulated for now.

Felspar was not altogether convinced and was contemplating his options whilst enjoying the pleasant sensation of Meredith's long red fingernails scratching the side of his jaw. As much as he enjoyed the attention, the black dragon was keen to be off. He wanted to stretch his wings again as he had been handicapped for so long recovering from his wounds. The memory made him shudder and pulling himself together he opened his red eyes.

"Very well… what is this important task you have for me!" he snarled.

Meredith paused for a second before replying as she weighed the dragon up carefully. They were like two predators circling each other; both attempting to out think and manoeuvre their opponent into a weaker position. But big and ferocious as Felspar was, Meredith was not scared. She had armed guards watching her at all times and they would not hesitate to use any means necessary to protect her.

"Have you heard of this object?" she replied showing him a drawing.

Felspar began to laugh.

"You lied woman... you *are* sending me on a fool's errand after all... that is an old myth with no substance what so ever!"

"That is where you are mistaken!" she replied coldly as she disliked being laughed at. "I have proof of its existence and of its probable whereabouts."

The black dragon stopped laughing and looked at Meredith with a calculated stare.

"How did you come about this information?"

"I told you before that I found what I needed in Calmor and the best part is that neither that fool Rathlin nor any of the others realise what they have there" she smiled indulgently.

"So tell me then, where do I find this precious artefact and what does it do?" he asked impatiently.

"You will have to travel to South East Asia to find it, my dear Felspar and let's just say that it will give us control over every dragon we encounter!"

Felspar considered her last statement and although he knew she really meant *she* would have control over any dragons they encountered, he still welcomed the diversion and would deal

with revenge later.

It did not take long for Meredith to explain the details to him as she did not have much information to go on, but he listened and would investigate the potential region when he got there. With not so much as a word he turned towards the doors, which opened at the touch of a button hidden under Meredith's desk. The dragon disappeared through the door to exit the building using a large hatch she had specially made for just such a winged visitor. Meredith watched him leave and expelled a breath with more force than a sigh. It was a constant battle to keep this dragon in check, but she was relieved that he had complied with her wishes for now. She pushed the button again to close the doors and walked to the window where a glass case stood. While Felspar disappeared into the afternoon sky she drummed her fingernails on the glass case containing one of her company's drilling rigs and smiled to herself. She had another plan for getting what she wanted and it did not involve the hotheaded dragon… not just yet anyway.

Chapter 4

'A Chilly Reception'

Angus only just managed to grip the saddle in time as Pyrra's unexpected manoeuvre threatened to unseat the young protector. He found himself upside down as the boats tourist passengers gaped at the magnificent city around them and fortunately, not at the two thousand year old dragon flying past them at high speed with a teenage lad on her back. A dragon's ability to make itself invisible to all but a true believer in the possession of Dragonore was indeed a very handy trick; one that had kept dragons safe from humans for thousands of years.

As the boat slipped away behind them, Pyrra righted, much to Angus' relief, and began to sweep towards a large statue.

"Sorry about that! Are you okay?" asked Pyrra with a hint of embarrassment in her voice.

"Totally… That was pretty cool!" replied Angus cheerily. He had quickly recovered from the event and it was yet another near miss that had become a regular occurrence in his life since meeting Pyrra.

"Wicked, there's the Statue of Liberty!" called Angus, "Do you know why it's green?" shouted the excited boy as they swooped down the East River and into the Hudson Harbour.

"It's painted that colour is it not?" the dragon surmised.

"No, it's made of bronze and according to the guide book she turned green in less than a year due to being outside in the elements."

Admittedly the dragon was both surprised and amused by this information.

"Perhaps I was originally bronze too!" she laughed.

As they sped across the bay Angus saw many boats and ferries of all shapes and sizes. Some carried more tourists like the ferry they had just narrowly missed and others appeared full of people on their way to work in the city. Pyrra slowed slightly and flew over a large barge being pushed by a bright red tug. The barge was full of waste and all kinds of rubbish, escorted by hundreds of seagulls. Pyrra had made the pair invisible before she dove under the bridge and one or two of the birds bounced off her body as she passed. Once they had overtaken the barge they wished they had steered clear as the stench was overwhelming.

"What a horrible smell" growled Pyrra, "How can the men in that tug put up with that at this time in the morning?"

Angus wanted to answer but he had pulled up his jacket over

his nose and did not want to expose his face. Pyrra gave a massive flap of her wings in an attempt to push the rubbish barge behind them more quickly and aimed towards the green statue and Liberty Island.

The massive statue loomed over them and Pyrra spiralled around the body a few times as she climbed in height towards the head of New York's most famous lady. Angus thought it was very cool to be able to see the statue in this way and realised how lucky he was to have his very own private tour. They continued their ascent until they were face to face with the formidable head of the statue. Angus looked into the famous sombre face and wondered at the engineering that must have gone into building such a structure.

"Where are we meeting Chad?" asked Pyrra, waking Angus from his reverie.

"He asked us to meet him near Little Italy" replied the lad grasping for his back pack, "I have a map in here somewhere!"

"Good, you navigate the way and I'll try not to hit any more ships!" she replied cheerfully.

Angus laughed at her joke as he thumbed his way through the map section of the guidebook. Within seconds they were off, following the instructions he shouted out.

The green dragon drove forward towards Manhattan, but kept higher to avoid the busy shipping lanes below. Angus directed her higher still, to allow him to view the streets from above. A dragon's eye view!

"Down there Pyrra, across the park and up that street between the two large sky scrapers" he pointed.

Before he knew it she was already above the traffic that filed through the busy streets of lower Manhattan and Angus could now hear the noise of the city. He realised it had always been present in the background, but now that they were closer to the tall buildings the sound was much more prominent. He narrowed his eyes in concentration and tried to isolate some of the urban sounds. At first it was difficult but then the noise of sirens began to filter through the general din and soon he was able to pick out the echoing wail of different sirens from various directions. Car horns blared and honked as busy New Yorkers made their way to offices and workplaces throughout the Wall Street financial area. Opening his eyes Angus looked down to see the sidewalks were filled with people going about their business and he had never seen such a busy place in all his life. Remembering his navigation task he checked the street name and called out the next set off instructions to Pyrra.

"What street is this?" asked the dragon.

"Broadway!" replied Angus still checking the map.

"It's very long!" called Pyrra.

"Yeah I guess it is..." said Angus looking into the distance. The building seemed to go on forever like a wall on either side of the road. Angus looked at the next street name and realised they were about to miss their turn.

"Turn right here!" he called out.

Pyrra spread her wings out wide and quickly made sharp turn towards a small park with a large building in the centre.

"Chad will meet us over there" said Angus pointing to a rather stately looking building with pillars in front of it.

The dragon pulled up sharply and landed in the square in front of New York City Hall folding her wings around her.

The square was almost empty Angus looked around and could see one or two people sitting wrapped up against the weather, on the benches under the large oak trees that dominated the park in front of City Hall. He wondered why more people did not enjoy the park and then he realised. When he was with Pyrra he was always warm as she could radiate heat through her scales. She had done this for him once before and she must have been doing that all the way over from Calmor. Now that he was no longer sitting on her back he could feel the

winter chill permeating through his clothes and he pulled his jacket zip fully up in reaction to the cold. Although dry, the December winter in New York was very much like home and a slight wind only served to emphasise the cold.

"When will Chad get here?" asked Pyrra having a look around.

"About nine..." replied Angus looking up at the clock tower, "we're ten minutes early!"

The young protector decided to wait on the steps leading up to the City Hall while Pyrra explored her new surroundings a little more. He made himself as comfortable as he could and chuckled as the green dragon studied the architecture of the building before ambling off to stare intently at a rubbish bin. She stood for some time turning her head to the side and looking at the receptacle from various angles. Angus was trying to understand why she found it so interesting when a young man stopped near the bin. He finished eating his breakfast before balling up the wrapper and throwing it into the bin. The paper spun through the air in a perfect trajectory but what he did not see was the invisible green dragon blocking the way. The young man was about to walk off when he saw the paper suddenly stop in mid air and drop straight to the ground. Only Angus could see Pyrra, and he grinned when he saw the total confusion on the man's face. As the dragon continued to study the bin the man went up to the paper and picked it up. He looked at the scrunched up wrapper puzzled as to how he missed his intended target. Angus watched as Pyrra moved to one side leaving the way clear. Shaking his head the man carefully tossed the wrapper into the bin again, but just as he did Pyrra's tail swished up as she turned to move off in the direction of an empty park bench. The paper struck her tail and flipped over the bin and onto the grass causing Angus to burst out laughing. The young protector watched as the man threw his arms up in the air and strode to the other side of the bin to retrieve the ball of paper. He looked at it closely turning it over and over in his hands with a most frustrated look on his face. Pyrra was now inspecting the bench by lifting it up at one end to look underneath it. Angus checked to ensure no one had seen the bench lift up but fortunately the only other human was the young man still scratching his head in puzzlement. The young lad had to cover his mouth to stifle his amusement when the man stepped forward to very carefully place the paper into the bin. Even after doing this he backed away carefully watching to see if the piece of paper would jump out the bin in some bizarre way! Angus laughed for some time after the man

finally turned and strode off very quickly. Even then he glanced back every now and then towards the bin.

"What are you laughing at?" asked Chad looking at Angus strangely.

"Oh hi Chad… Nothing really," replied Angus taken by surprise, "Didn't see you arrive."

Chad had grown almost as much as Angus had in the past few months and being a little older was showing the signs of manhood in the form of sparse stubble on his chin.

"You been waiting long?" asked the bigger lad.

"Not really, Pyrra is just taking in the sights" he answered by looking in her direction and then burst out laughing at the sight of her rattling an iron railing just as a woman was walking past. The poor woman, on seeing the railing move rapidly all on its own sped up rapidly in an effort to put some distance between her and the strange occurrence.

Chad chuckled as the dragon made her way over to the young protectors. He wished Macklin was a little more like Pyrra and not the grumpy and hot tempered beast that made life difficult whenever the opportunity arose.

"Chad! How are you?" called Pyrra as she dodged a couple of pedestrians crossing the square.

"I'm cool" replied the larger boy, "What about you?"

"Yes I'm cool too... in fact it's positively freezing here" she replied seriously, "do you think it will snow?"
Both Angus and Chad doubled up laughing and Pyrra, who did not see the joke, stood indignantly looking from one to the other.

"Well I don't see what's so funny about that!"
Eventually they managed to stop laughing, although the occasional muffled titter still emanated from one or the other of them.

Chad explained that Macklin would not come to meet them but he was in fact only a couple of blocks away. They decided to walk to his hiding place as Angus was keen to get a closer look at the city from the ground. Pyrra took off and followed from the air as the two boys sauntered out of the square exchanging news. Chad was keen to hear about time travel and the adventure Angus had since their last meeting in Krubera. The pair talked animatedly as they made their way onto Centre Street and into the throng of pedestrians. They kept left and crossed the road towards a strange looking building that turned out to be the Civic Centre. On the way past Angus noticed a large black spike across the busy street; it was in the middle of a fountain directly in front of the Civic

Centre. He stopped telling Chad about the Vikings for a second and stood in wonder taking in the sights, sounds and smells of Lower Manhattan. Yellow taxis honked, road signs flashed 'walk/don't walk', and steam rose from vents in the pavement beneath them. A small cart near the ground clock also had steam rising from it; Angus sniffed the air and the smell of pretzels and hot dogs filled his nostrils from this street vendor. As they progressed further and turned right Angus noticed the buildings began to take on a more oriental theme. All manner of bright neon signs flashed and blinked from many of the buildings. New York really was a vibrant city but it also seemed very modern and Angus wondered could there really be dragons here? It was an unlikely place to inhabit, even for the most extrovert dragon he knew, which was of course Cyru. But then he did not know Macklin very well, having only seen him briefly at the Trials. The red dragon was the reason they had come to New York on SSDP business. His native New Yorker protector Chad was having trouble with the red dragon, but Angus had no idea what that trouble entailed. He had already tuned in to Chad's soft American drawl and understood that the dragon's place of Hibernation on some building had become the middle of a construction project as they were digging up the roads and laying cables all around. The noise of the pneumatic drills and diggers was driving the dragon demented and Chad was worried the short tempered dragon would do something silly.

"He's really angry and can't sleep..." explained Chad, "and there are not so many places to hide a dragon in New York." The protector really had no idea what to do and had tried persuading the red dragon to move Upstate, but Macklin was proving very difficult and refused to be relocated.

As they strolled up Walker Street, Chad pointed ahead and Angus could see the red and white barriers with their yellow flashing warning lights all over the road signalling the construction area. A variety of heavy vehicles worked on the resurfacing as more trucks stood by filled with materials ready for the next stage of road construction. Further on, the New York Electrical Company were feeding large cables into a hole in the ground. Angus followed the red painted lines that signified the next trench to be dug and it stretched all the way up to an information booth with a large wooden dragon on the roof. The box was red like Macklin and the wooden dragon on top was carved in the shape of a traditional Chinese style dragon. Pyrra landed next to the booth just as Macklin morphed from it.

"Why are you here?" he wheeled on Chad who visibly cringed as if scared he was about to be eaten. "Did *you* invite them?"

Chapter 5

'Park Life

Angus and Chad spent an hour trying to calm the irate red dragon and assuring him that no conspiracy had been plotted against him. This was made all the more difficult because they could barely make themselves heard over the sound of the construction workers digging the road near the little information booth. Pyrra eventually persuaded Macklin to see reason, but the soon to be evicted dragon was extremely cantankerous and ungrateful for the proffered help; no doubt due to lack of sleep these past few weeks.

"I don't understand why the SSDP cannot simply halt the construction. The idea of re-housing me is all too inconvenient for words" moaned Macklin.

"Do you have any preference about where you'd like to live?" asked Angus, patiently.

"I do not wish to move!" snarled the dragon stubbornly.

"Okay... what about The Empire State Building?" asked Angus patiently, "At least let's find a temporary arrangement..."

"Why would I want to live way up there!" grumbled Macklin unhelpfully and clearly in no mood to cooperate.

Angus looked at Chad for some help but it was obvious that he did not have any ideas on how to appease the obstinate dragon.

"Why don't we do a bit of sightseeing and maybe we'll find something?" suggested Angus in an attempt to humour the dragon and to manufacture an opportunity to see more of the splendid city.

The dragons and the two boys took to the skies to scan the city from above and decide where they wanted to go first. As they rose through the street level the noise of the traffic began to mingle with other urban sounds. By now it was midday and the city that never sleeps was very much in full swing. Lingering Christmas decorations still glittered in the waning winter sunlight as they cleared the lower rooftops of the Manhattan skyline. Angus had an idea of where he wanted to go first, and the higher they flew, the more certain he became. The Empire State Building was one of the most dominant landmarks of the New York skyline and Angus was extremely keen to see it.

"What about that?" he suggested, pointing towards the tall sky scraper.

After a brief discussion with Macklin, Chad shrugged his shoulders and gave an exasperated nod of agreement.

Sweeping upwards Angus could see that the observation deck swarmed with tourists. This was going to be a tricky landing, but then higher up he noticed a smaller deck with very few people on it. They landed unseen on what turned out to be the 102nd floor and Angus marvelled at the architecture and height of the building from a new perspective. To think that men built this tower at a time when modern machinery was unavailable totally amazed him. Chad gazed out through the barrier looking decidedly bored and Angus realised he had probably seen the view many times before. Macklin was sitting against the tower picking his teeth with a claw with a look of complete contempt both for his companions and the situation he found himself in. Pyrra was holding onto the top of the high barrier and had craned her neck over the side.

"Look at all these people below… why do humans build such high structures when they do not have wings?"

"To save space I guess" replied Angus as he joined her. To say he was excited by the tremendous views was an understatement. Words failed him as he gazed all the way around New York, laid out in panorama. To the south he saw Wall Street and the famous Flatiron building as well as the poignant Ground Zero where the World Trade Centre's twin towers

once stood. As he walked around the viewing platform, the famous sports venue, Madison Square Garden was visible; then the Statue of Liberty and Ellis Island all came into view on the west side. To the north he could see right up 5th Avenue to Central Park. Eastwards held the Manhattan and Brooklyn bridges and then on to Queens, Brooklyn and Long Island. Immediately below him he marvelled at the famous art deco Chrysler Building with its golden spire.

Coming back to reality and refocusing on the task in hand Angus turned his attention to the majestic building they now stood on.

"Have you checked it out for a hiding place?" he asked Chad.

"Yeah… Nothing for Macklin to morph into up here" replied Chad gloomily.

"Well it may be good enough for giant gorillas, but no hiding places for an old dragon!" added the red dragon huffily. Angus realised he was referring to Hollywood's legendary King Kong, but the red dragon was correct and even with the greatest imagination he could see that there really was nothing remotely dragon themed in the vicinity. Macklin's mood seemed to darken again and even Pyrra looked glum.

"Well what about Lady Liberty herself then?" she asked.

"I suppose we can have a look if we must!" replied Macklin in the tone of a spoilt child.
Chad thought it best to humour him and he jumped on his back as the pair led the way. Macklin hopped onto the heavy guard rail and then plunged off the top of the Empire State Building straight down past the tourists and into the busy New York streets. Pyrra followed in the same manner and Angus felt the adrenalin course through his body as she swooped into the street below and sped after Macklin.

The red dragon swung from side to side in the street, as if toying with the many buildings that lined 5th Avenue. Macklin came so close at one point that Angus thought he would surely clip a street sign that protruded from one of the upper floors of an old grey stone building. Suddenly he changed course and they gained height leaving the sounds of the traffic fading below them as they swept over the rooftops towards the harbour. As they flew over Ellis Island Angus remembered something he had read in the guidebook before leaving Calmor. He pondered how many immigrants had ascended the famous staircases to either a new life in America or passage back home on the same ship that brought them had they been unfortunate enough to fail the selection process. Both dragons

alighted on the Statue of Liberty's crown and the boys carefully climbed down on top of the head. They gingerly made their way to the edge of the crown and looked out in amazement at the Manhattan skyline before them. At least Chad was not bored now as even he a native New Yorker had not managed to take in the city from this viewpoint.

"Now this is more like it… a proper location befitting my station. Maybe I could live here" suggested Macklin, "and spook the tourists" he added with a touch of humour; the first Angus had ever heard in his voice.

"Where would you hide?" asked Pyrra.

"Well perhaps in the torch, we both spout flames!" said Macklin sarcastically.

But even he had to admit that this was no more suitable for him than the Empire State building. Angus understood from Pyrra that Dragons could technically morph into anything, but she told him they needed something dragon themed to make it easier to achieve and neither this site nor the Empire State offered anything really suitable.

"I've had enough of this… I'm going back to my booth" the red dragon moaned like a petulant child, "Those noisy road workers break for lunch around now, so I'll get a bit of peace for a while."

Before anyone could say a word Macklin had taken off and left poor Chad standing on the top of the Statue of Liberty.

"Well of all the…" began Pyrra.

"I know and I'm sorry" said Chad quickly, "but this is actually his idea of a joke!"

"Well he has a really strange sense of humour and I will be having words when we catch up with him!"

Angus saw the pained expression on Chad's face and decided to redirect Pyrra's attention, sensing the young American's embarrassment at being stranded by his dragon.

"Why don't we go see some more landmarks first?"

Pyrra agreed, and declared that they had all had enough sulking for one day and invited both boys onto her back before taking flight once more. Angus took another long look, committing to memory the famous lady standing resolutely on Liberty Island; the gateway to America, a symbol and promise of a new home for so many immigrants over the years.

Chad sitting in front of Angus directed Pyrra to Columbus Circle on the edge of Central Park and the boys decided to hire bikes for a couple of hours so they could cycle round the whole of the vast park. Pyrra found this highly amusing as she could cover the park in approximately five minutes by air, but she had to remind herself that they were teenage boys and that sometimes flying on the back of a dragon was not always as exciting as it sounded. She took off and kept an eye on them as they happily freewheeled below her. They had agreed to signal her and meet up somewhere in the middle of the park.

The pathways and tracks were full of joggers; mothers pushing strollers and other pedestrians wrapped up against the chill and enjoying the winter sunshine. Angus looked to the sky as Pyrra wheeled acrobatically above. All of these human beings in one place and every one of them oblivious to the fact that there was a great green dragon circling overhead.

"Chad, do you know how Wall Street got its name?" shouted Angus to the local lad.

"Course... we learned that in Elementary, the Dutch

recommended its construction back in the 1600's. The Wall was supposed to keep your British Navy out of our harbour!" he added, laughing.

"So what's good to see here in the park?"

"Dunno… I guess the boating lake is worth a look and then maybe the zoo" suggested Chad looking much happier now that Macklin was not around.

Angus nodded in agreement and they began to race each other through the large park.

The boats proved to be a great idea and they both had a go at rowing using the wooden oars. They soon managed to get the hang of it but not before they collided with another boat that contained three girls. The girls were having terrible trouble steering their small rowing boat and even managed to lose an oar. Angus and Chad gallantly retrieved the lost object from the water and returned it to the grateful girls. Angus watched Chad chat easily with them and noted to himself that one of them bore a slight resemblance to Georgina. It had only been a couple of days since he last saw her but already he was missing his next closest friend to Pyrra.

The zoo proved to be a little dull although Chad was pleased to bump into the girls again and this time he managed to exchange cell phone numbers with the most giggly of the trio.

They cycled on through the park and Angus wondered what else they could do. They had still not found anything remotely like a dragon hiding place and the day was wearing on. Some of the hills were now getting a bit hard going and they eventually came to an outdoor theatre. It was closed but something else caught Angus' eye.

"Let's try up there" he pointed.

Chad shrugged and pushed off in the direction indicated by the sign Angus had spotted. They puffed up the last slope to a small but rather impressive looking castle perched above a small lake. Angus stopped to read the sign and he read about the castle's renovation and restoration.

"Belvedere Castle… did you know this was here?" asked Angus.

"No… never heard of it!" replied Chad looking over the wall and into the pond.

Angus looked around the surroundings and started to feel a little cold.

"Let's go and see what's inside."

The boys abandoned their bikes and raced through the door and up the stairs to get a look at the view across Turtle Pond. The castle certainly suited its name, which meant 'beautiful view', but this building really was a Victorian folly; a fantasy castle meant only to enhance the landscape. It had never been lived in and was nothing more than a scenic lookout. Belvedere Castle was now used to observe nature and as a weather station. It amused the boys to think the custodians would freak out big time if they knew they had a real live dragon in their midst! After taking in the scenery for a while they decided it was time to return to the bikes and get back. Outside, Angus turned and studied the small castle once more, just as he had done with the Statue of Liberty. When he looked at the door he laughed so loudly and so suddenly that it startled Chad.

"What is it?" he asked.

"Look above the door!" replied Angus as he signalled to Pyrra hovering overhead.

The green dragon quickly landed beside the boys and followed Angus' outstretched arm pointing towards the small castle. She saw the item they had missed in their eagerness to get up the stairs. The perfect hiding place for a dragon!

Chapter 6

'Trouble at home'

It did not take the boys long to check the bikes in, and as they jumped onto Pyrra's back Angus heard the wailing sound of siren's echoing through the streets. As they rose, the source of the blaring became apparent as three fire trucks sped past on a nearby road.

"Follow them Pyrra!" shouted Chad.

With hardly a pause she was bearing down on the last of the fire trucks as it weaved through the traffic following the two in front. With NYFD badges emblazoned on the doors, the bright red body of the truck gleamed even in the dull winter sunshine. Angus noticed that the truck was so long it had a fireman sitting at the back to help with the steering. With its long silver ladder lying flat on top, it looked like a serpent as it slithered between the cars on the road. Their excitement rose as they continued to follow; only to feel guilt at this euphoria when they remembered that these firemen were probably on their way to save someone in danger. Suddenly the fire trucks screeched to a halt next to a burning building, two floors were engulfed in flames and the fire crew immediately jumped from the cabins and began working efficiently on various tasks. Angus marvelled at the way every person in the crew knew their job so well and each was fully aware of what the person next to them would do. Like clockwork, one team had entered the building while another had extended the long ladder, hoses spraying water into the flaming building in an effort to contain the blaze. Police cars had blocked the street to stop onlookers getting in the way and ambulance crews stood by to deal with any casualties. Angus could not help think that it was exciting to watch, like a scene in a movie, until he caught sight of a man at a window on the topmost floor of the apartment block. The flames from the floors below were getting closer to him and the smoke from the fire was pouring out through the window, silhouetting the trapped man. The fire crew that had entered the building now reappeared carrying or helping many of the residents from the burning building. More fire trucks arrived to spray water into the flaming apartments, but all eyes were on the man at the window as he climbed precariously onto the ledge in what looked like a hopeless attempt to escape the heat and flames that would surely engulf him. The crew swung the end of the ladder which quickly rose, in an effort to aid the soot blackened man. A fireman stood on top, ready to give aid.

"They won't be able to reach him!" shouted

Chad from behind Angus.

The American dragon protector was correct and it became apparent very quickly that the fire crews had run out of ideas. The flames were now spewing from the windows next to the man and Angus could see the desperate look on his face as he looked desperately towards the ladder two floors below him.

"Pyrra he's going to jump… we need to do something!" shouted Angus.

Already thinking ahead, his green scaled friend had started to move just as the man leapt from the ledge. It was plain to all that he had severely misjudged the jump and should have missed by several feet; but somehow the ladder moved. At least that is how it looked to those watching below. What had actually happened was the intervention of Pyrra. She had just managed to catch the man's leg and moved him enough to ensure he caught the top of the ladder. Only then did she let go and fly to a safer distance from the scene. The gathering crowd cheered and applauded as the fire crew brought the man safely to the ground.

The heroic firemen soon brought the fire under control but the threesome had already left to find Macklin and it seemed they arrived just in the nick of time. The red dragon was not asleep in his hiding place which is what they had expected; he was morphed and towering menacingly over a bunch of workmen. The men were gathered around a small crane looking bemused and thoroughly confused. Angus and Chad dropped off from Pyrra and managed to stay undetected as her invisibility power extended to them while she was close.

"Look buddy, this crane was working five minutes ago and there's no reason on earth why it don't work now!" shouted a big man very loudly to a smaller man in a white helmet. Angus could see that the bigger man was probably the driver of the crane and it looked like the white helmeted man was in charge of the construction work. The others just seemed to be enjoying the show.

"Well it ain't working now, is it?" replied the small foreman rather testily. "Look pal all I know is I gotta get this booth moved today and you're all I got... so get it working and get on with it!"

The big man looked furiously at the small man for a second or two both in the shadow of the dragon, and Angus felt sure he was going to say something rude, but instead he stomped back to his crane and climbed up into the cabin. The crane lumbered into life and the jib swung round as the other workmen grabbed the slings that had been attached to the booth. As the

long arm of the crane swung towards the booth Macklin stepped forward and used his head and horns to push against the cranes progress. The machinery strained noisily as it laboured against the strength of the invisible dragon and it reminded Angus of an arm wrestling match he had once seen. This went on for a minute or so until the foreman stepped forward and waved the crane operator to stop his useless attempt to shift the crane.

Angus and Chad turned to Pyrra as this was not a situation the young humans felt equipped to deal with and the green dragon cautiously approached Macklin, who still had his head butted against the crane.

"Macklin this is futile… they will get the booth eventually!" she whispered into his ear.

"I know…" he strained, "but I'm not giving up without a fight!"

"It's okay! You don't have to…" she replied, "The boys have found you an excellent new home."

She had his attention now and Angus could see that he had lessened the pressure against the crane and it moved a few inches closer to its target.

"Seriously?" he tried to ask as he re-applied his push.

"Absolutely… and much better than this… protected by

humans and with no workmen in sight" she said teasing the belligerent dragon.

As the larger red dragon contemplated Pyrra's statement, the crane driver was now telling the foreman that the crane was working fine and that since it had just moved he could get it all the way.

Without a word Macklin removed his head and the crane swung past unhindered to its target. The sudden release of pressure had caught the operator unaware and he fought to regain control of the vehicle. Macklin stepped aside with Pyrra as the men swarmed over the booth like worker ants attaching the slings.

"I hope you're right about this Pyrra!" growled the red dragon.

"I assure you Macklin, you will not be disappointed" she replied coolly.

The protectors mounted up and set off for Central Park again and watched as Macklin's home was lifted onto a waiting truck.

The fiery red dragons mood appeared to worsen the closer they flew to Central Park. Angus could see that Chad was explaining where they were going but whatever he said only seemed to anger Macklin more. They touched down near the

small castle and walked toward the entrance.

"So where is this wonderful new home then?" grumbled Macklin.

Angus just simply pointed in the direction of the entrance and there, over the door, was a plate casting of a wyvern, weather worn and green in colour. Pyrra and the two lads stood with some trepidation in the forlorn hope the ever angry dragon would approve his new lodging.

"Well I don't think much of the colour... I preferred my red booth..." predictably grumbled the red dragon.

Pyrra audibly sighed and was about to speak when.

"But I think it will do... even if it is a Wyvern!" growled Macklin quietly under his breath.

Angus had to almost pinch his own arm and Chad was stunned so much his jaw was hanging down. Suddenly they all burst out laughing and congratulated each other on the fact that Macklin was now safely relocated and would hopefully be a lot happier.

Angus was to stay at Chad's house for a night before the long flight home but first he had some presents to buy. Chad pointed him in the direction of a reputable souvenir shop so he could do a bit of shopping. The young protector chose a snow globe of Times Square for Aurora Tek and a rather obvious 'I love New York' t-shirt for Georgina. As he paid for the gifts he remembered he had promised to phone Calmor Castle to update the Teks on the outcome of Macklin's situation.

Five minutes later he was tapping the number pad of the payphone and waited patiently for the line to connect. The line was good but it took both parties some time to adjust to the time delay.

"Angus my boy we've been waiting for your call, are you okay?" cried Rathlin down the phone and making the common mistake that the greater the distance meant the louder the caller had to shout.

"I'm fine Rathlin and we've managed to find a new home for Macklin!" replied Angus.

"Already… excellent!" shouted Rathlin, "But I'm afraid we've had a rather unfortunate development here…"

Angus missed the last part of the sentence as a

traffic jam had produced a volley of car horns blaring behind him and he was forced to stick his finger in his other ear in an effort to block out the sounds from the streets of the city that never sleeps.

"Come again?" shouted Angus.

The young protector finally got the rest of the message.

"We're on our way… Bye!" he said before banging the receiver quickly back on the cradle and ending the call.

Ashen faced the young lad turned to Pyrra.

"We have to return to Calmor immediately… sorry Chad, something terrible has happened!"

Chapter 7

'Mysterious Disappearance'

Rathlin Tek, head of The Secret Society of Dragon Protectors sat in front of his satellite link to Krubera, and was updating Ward Godroi on the situation. The Ward was the guardian of the Cor Stan; the precious and ancient rock which gave all dragons their special powers and was the only source of Dragonore. The satellite communication system had been a gift from Meredith and the encryption codes had been changed since her departure to ensure that no one could hack into their private discussions with Krubera.

"Good morning Godroi… Finian…" he said quickly exchanging greetings with his brother.
Finian lived in the deep cave system at Krubera with Godroi and he was the Ward's protector.

"Any sign of them?" asked Finian tersely.

"I'm afraid not…" replied Rathlin sadly shaking his head, "But we did manage to speak to Angus though!"

"Excellent…" exclaimed Godroi, "How is he getting on?"

"He's completed the task and is on his way back now" answered Rathlin.

"Well that was fast work but I fear the journey back will be too much for Pyrra if she has not rested properly!" added Godroi concerned for her safety, "In fact too much for any dragon!"

"You underestimate Pyrra's strength and we all know how Angus is; they were quite insistent!"

"I bet they were!" added Finian, "When do you expect them?"

"Assuming they are okay, anytime soon…" said Rathlin just as a terrible wail emanated from the background, like a dragon in mortal pain. "Poor girl is not coping too well with the loss… I'd better go and see what's happening."

The white haired man disappeared from the screen forgetting to turn it off and left Godroi and Finian wondering what on earth they could do to help.

Angus and Pyrra were exhausted having flown non-stop from New York and even as direct as the dragon flew this was still an arduous journey through serious weather systems. They entered Calmor Castle through the secret underground passage and Pyrra touched down just inside the great doors of the main cavern. Already they could sense that the mood within the castle was sombre and indeed a black cloud hung over the remote island as if nature itself was in sympathy with the plight of the distraught red dragon.

Pyrra sank to the floor just as soon as she reached the main underground cavern and Angus, his limbs exceedingly stiff from the flight, gratefully slid to the ground. Rathlin and Aurora Tek, the owners of the castle were there to greet them with faces almost as sad as poor Rhys.

"Pyrra you look exhausted, are you all right dear?" clucked Mrs Tek as she approached the prone dragon.

"I'm… fine…" panted Pyrra, "Just need… a good night's… sleep!"

"Angus my boy, what about you?" asked Rathlin.

"I'm fine but Pyrra really had to work hard to get back" he replied as he stroked her head, "The storm was just as bad as on the way there!"

"Well you're here now and that's all that matters!" said Rathlin.

"So what happened?" asked Angus eagerly.

"Well we don't really know dear" explained Aurora Tek, "Rhys had checked on the eggs before she went out to stretch her wings" she shook her head sadly, tears welling in her eyes "Poor Argent had offered to keep an eye on them while she went out with Swithin… Oh I'm sorry, but it's just so

terrible!"

She pulled a handkerchief from her sleeve like a magician and began to dab the tears from her cheeks. Rathlin put his arm around his wife's shoulder affectionately and continued filling them in on the terrible discovery.

"Well the first we knew of anything being amiss was yesterday morning when Rhys and Swithin returned. Poor Argent was asleep on the job and Rhys' screams woke everyone up!"

"Didn't Argent hear or see anything?" asked Angus.

"No and worst still there were no clues" replied Rathlin, "It's as if a ghost took them!"

"Those poor little dragons will hatch and who knows what will happen to them!" wailed Mrs Tek.

Nothing more needed to be said and as to the whereabouts of the eggs, the first to be laid since the beginning of the Great Hibernation; no one had any clue where to start looking. Rathlin's reminder that the eggs were due to hatch in a little over a week, further highlighted the seriousness and urgency of the matter.

Poor Rhys was emitting a terrible keening sound quite unlike anything Angus had ever heard before. It was a sort of high pitched vibrating noise, a continuous droning.

"There, there Rhys, do not fret..." said Pyrra as she tried to comfort her, "we will get them back before you know it."

"But they will not hatch unless I keep warming them!" wailed the distraught dragon.

"I know but at least they won't hatch without you there and you can reheat them to encourage them to hatch once we find them..."

"You can find them Pyrra... can't you?" interrupted Rhys, "You and Angus always know what to do..." she turned to Angus and gripped his shoulder desperately with her right fore claw, "You can do it Angus, you are Dracagast!"

Angus was not often scared of a dragon but the deranged look in Rhys' eyes was enough to quell any spirit. Pyrra managed to pry the claw from the lad's shoulder before any damage was done and she led Rhys away to a small cave whispering soothing words as she went; whilst the red dragon stared back at Angus until she was led out of sight.

Angus was very disturbed by the state of Rhys and she was a far cry from the beautiful and proud mother to be he had seen only days before. After Pyrra caught up with him he discovered what appeared to be upsetting the red dragon more than anything was that without a mother's warming flame the fire

whelps would not grow properly inside the eggs. They would eventually grow cold and hibernate just like an adult dragon. This meant they could not hatch and the longer they stayed cold the more time it would take to heat them up again.

"So they would almost turn to stone?" asked Angus incredulously.

"Exactly!" confirmed Pyrra, "And that's why Swithin, their poor father, is out looking for them now!"

Everyone was at a loss to know what to say or do. Worse still it appeared that all expectations had been pinned on Angus and Pyrra's return; as if they would come up with a solution and save the day. Angus knew they had managed to do so on previous occasions, but more often than not he had been lucky, or had the help of the strange dragon in his dreams. Unfortunately he had not had anything like those dreams for months and he was beginning to feel frustrated. How was he ever going to find the eggs when no one had any clues!

As soon as they were recovered enough from their long journey, Angus and Pyrra flew around the dragons in the locality to spread the terrible news and recruited as much assistance for the search as possible. Swithin had done his best to cover as much ground as he could, but the father was now exhausted and as incapable of logical thought as Rhys.

Angus and Pyrra put their knowledge of all the hidden dragons to work and began to systematically visit as many as they could; spreading the news of the loss to the shocked dragon community.

Two days had passed and still the search proved fruitless and as the New Year rapidly approached, the mood on Calmor Island was not a happy one. Angus had been invited to go on a trip to London with Georgina and her father and he knew Pyrra needed a rest, but before he set off he knew they had one more call to make. They landed near the main gate of the estate and walked to the majestic gateway flanked by two stone dragons looking down on those who dared approach. They both called out the name of Caedmon but no answer came forth and from the lack of warmth and glow of their Dragonore it was apparent he was no longer there. Angus had to admit they were an excellent place to hide a dragon and it seemed a pity that neither gatepost was occupied.

"He must have moved on as he had promised he would" said Pyrra. "Shall we

go in then?"
Angus nodded in agreement and then stopped after a few paces away from the gate.

"I wonder if Meredith is at home?" he said, deliberating.

"Why would we want to speak to her?" asked Pyrra making her distaste for the women plain.

"Why not?" replied Angus. "I'm sure she has a grudge against all of us and I wouldn't put it past her, would you?"
It was a logical argument and Pyrra had to agree with her young protector.

They flew up the drive and landed on the enormous front lawn of the estate looking up at the mansion, which was the ancestral home of the Quinton-Jones family. Meredith had inherited a vast wealth from her father as well as many companies, some of which bore the family name. Angus jumped down and began to look through windows in the hope he would spot her or even better, the stolen eggs.

"I guess no one is home" said Pyrra, her neck stretched to peer into one of the upper windows.
The lad did not answer and not wishing to give up on his tenuous hope, he kept looking in window after window.

"Might I enquire as to what you think you are doing young sir?" said a voice from behind Angus.

Both he and Pyrra spun round and Angus realised he had put too much distance between himself and Pyrra and so he was highly visible. The man before him wore a crisp uniform and his haughty demeanour suggested to Angus that he would not be easily fooled. Angus admonished himself for the lapse in concentration that had made him visible and thus allowing what appeared to be a butler to see him.

"I… I'm looking for Meredith" he blustered.

"Most guests of Miss Quinton-Jones enter via the front door at the appointed time" added the man curtly, "I presume you do have an appointment or shall I be calling the police?"

The man was smiling but nothing about the smile was friendly and Angus sensed that Pyrra was becoming rather agitated. He decided to bluff it out.

"Yes she is expecting me and I just got a little lost!" he answered, hoping he sounded confident.

The butler considered Angus for a second or two as if deciding whether or not to believe the young intruder.

"Well young sir, since the Mistress will no doubt be waiting for you I had better show you the way to her study!"

And with that, Angus was escorted to the very person he had intended to see. As they walked the butler placed his hand on the shoulder that Rhys had gripped a couple of days before and Angus wanted to pull away, but he also realised that would give the wrong impression. So instead he put up with the slight pain and allowed the butler to guide him into the stately home.

Meredith, resplendent in red trousers and a red cashmere sweater, stood inside a large room full with wall to wall books on one side and a large desk dominating the opposite wall. An ornate gold framed painting hung on the wall behind the desk and the young lad's eyes were drawn to the striking and stern and vaguely familiar image of an elderly man; the late Horace Quinton-Jones. Meredith was at the bookshelf and turned to face them when the butler coughed quietly to attract her attention. A look of slight surprise crossed her face momentarily, before she regained her composure and smiled without much warmth.

"My, my… to what do I owe the pleasure of this unexpected visit?" she asked.

"I'm sorry Mistress Meredith... but this… young man said he had an appointment!"

"Did he indeed!" she replied smiling thinly, "Well you had better leave him to me, thank you Millar."

Angus was not sure what to expect but he also knew the

welcome would not be pleasant. Meredith waited for Millar to leave as she walked over to the desk and sat perched on the front of it.

"Manners would normally dictate I should invite you to sit down but we both know you will not be staying long!" she fired in a clipped tone, no hint of a smile on her face, and Angus could not help but notice the resemblance she had to the portrait behind her.

"Don't worry… I won't take up too much of your time… I just have one question to ask you and then I will be off!" replied Angus just as curtly.

Meredith sized up the young man in front of her. It had been several months since she had last seen the lad and as children had a habit of doing at his age, he had noticeably grown taller.

"And what if I choose not to answer your question?" she replied.

"That's up to you, but I'll ask it anyway" added Angus unperturbed by the woman before him.

Again Meredith sized him up, just as she would a corporate businessman. 'He would make a great executive one day' she thought and in truth she admired the young protector for having the courage to come and see her.

"Ask away!" she said sharply.

Angus took a deep breath.

"Are you behind the theft of Rhys' dragon eggs?"

Complete silence met Angus for longer than he cared to count and he realised she was not going to answer him.

"So Rhys' eggs have been stolen, have they? How careless of your little club!" sneered Meredith.

It was more of a confirmation of his question than an answer.

"That was not an answer!" stated Angus.

"My apologies Angus, you are quite correct. The truth of the matter is I have absolutely no desire to have anything to do with dragons. I have other fish to fry."

Angus watched her carefully looking for any sign of a lie.

"I can not tell you I am sad about it, but I can assure you, I did not steal those eggs!" finished Meredith unblinkingly staring right into Angus' eyes.

Angus weighed up her response and decided that perhaps he had been clutching at straws by thinking she was the culprit. After all, the woman was seriously wealthy and had her many companies to run and manage. Now that he thought about it, what could she possibly hope to gain?

Meredith watched Angus walk out to the lawn and disappear from view. She went to her desk, took a small blue stone from the top drawer and returned to the window.

"Ah there she is" she said to herself.

The green dragon was never far from her little sidekick. The two appeared to be in discussion no doubt Pyrra was being told what had taken place. Angus shook his head as the green dragon said something to him and after a brief exchange he jumped up onto her back and they flew off. Apparently Angus had believed her and she had told the truth. She had not stolen the eggs!

Chapter 8

'A New Distraction'

As the duo flew from Meredith's family estate Angus could not help feeling a little disappointed that the ex protector had not proved to be the culprit. He chastised himself for being naïve enough to think he could waltz into her stately home and did he really expect to catch her red handed stroking the stolen eggs.

"You're very quiet" said Pyrra jostling him from his thoughts, "what's the matter?"

"Nothing really… Just thinking about things" replied Angus without much enthusiasm.

"Well not to worry, we will find the eggs soon and remember you've got a trip to London tomorrow with Georgina" encouraged the green dragon.

Angus brightened at the thought of seeing Georgina again as he had not managed to visit Marnham since his return from New York. This was mainly due to the intense search that had begun almost as soon as they had touched down in Calmor. He was sure that Pyrra would welcome the rest and he would certainly enjoy Georgina's company.

The Christmas holidays provided some free time for Angus

and Georgina to go to London with her father Hugh Penfold. He was a dragon protector as well as being the Vicar of St George's church in Marnham. Now that the Christmas services were over with he had promised to take the pair on a trip to London as he had some church business there. This meant taking the train rather than their more regular and unusual means of winged transport. The diversion of the trip gave them all time away from the anxieties and tensions of the current problem since almost every dragon and protector in the world now actively sought the missing eggs.

Pyrra was very keen to get to Marnham and they arrived much earlier than required for the train. Angus did not mind this as it allowed him more time with Georgina but he was unable to understand why Pyrra was so keen since Godroi now lived in Krubera and Argent had almost moved permanently to Calmor these days. It was not until the dragons exchanged greetings that he noticed that Pyrra seemed to be very friendly with Georgina's new dragon Wymarc. In fact he would say she was as much at ease with him as she was with Argent and Godroi. He made a mental note to ask the wily dragon about this new friendship when they were on their way home. Before moving indoors Angus stopped to stare at Wymarc as the tilt of his head

only seconds before had reminded him of something. He realised that in colouring, Wymarc reminded him of the strange blue dragon who invaded his sleep some months back, but he had not had any visitations for a while, not since they had managed to avert Godroi's death. As he watched the two dragons talking he dismissed it as no more than a trick of the light and followed Georgina into the house.

The young dragon protectors discussed the missing eggs and the lack of any clues to their whereabouts. Angus told Georgina about his visit to see Caedmon and his encounter with Meredith.

"Angus, tell me you didn't!" replied Georgina in shock. "That woman could have called the Police and had you arrested for trespassing or something."

Admittedly he had not thought too much about the consequences of his actions at the time but grudgingly admitted she was right.

"Well I thought she could have stolen them..." he half-heartedly offered in reply, "but at least we can rule her out now!" he added quickly, not wanting to dwell on his foolishness.

"I suppose so, but she could possibly have been lying to you" she replied teasingly.

"I watched her face carefully and it didn't look like she was

lying!" he replied rising to the bait.
Georgina just laughed at the look of utter indignation on his face and Angus seeing her smile began to laugh as he realised she had got him again with one of her teases. The subject soon changed to his recent visit to New York and Angus gave her the t-shirt and a detailed account of the sights they saw and Pyrra's timely intervention on behalf of the poor man who jumped from the burning building.

"Wow!" said Georgina for about the tenth time, "So what happened with Macklin?"
Angus continued with the story of how they found a new home for the red dragon but he tactfully left out the bit about meeting the girls on the boat.

It was not long after 8 o'clock when Hugh Penfold entered the living room; wiping crumbs of breakfast toast from his mouth and finding Angus and Georgina deep in conversation. They left for the railway station in the vicar's car after Angus phoned home to remind his parents that he was now off on his trip to London with the Penfolds. He smiled a wry smile as the Kleenware answer phone clicked on; clearly his parents would not be missing him then!

Seated on the London train, facing the direction of travel, Angus placed his head against the window and experimented with parallax. It was something he had learned in science at school and it was all to do with two observations of an object against a moving background. The object would change depending on how you looked at it. He watched the landscape pass by at speed if he put his head one way leaning on the window and much more slowly if he turned his head and looked forwards. Eventually the rhythmic sound of the tracks lulled him into a fitful sleep and strange images of the dragon eggs flitted through his mind. A sudden lurch from the carriage as the train stopped at another station caused him to awaken with a start. Angus quickly regained his wits and glanced over at Georgina who was doing a Suduko puzzle in her father's newspaper. The vicar slept, his jaw dropping open as he snored gently and Angus noticed that Georgina had her elbow expertly positioned to maintain her father in an upright position as he comically nodded sideways in her direction every few minutes or so.

The city grew around the train as it progressed closer to the centre of London; the sound from the tracks changed tempo as the train traversed diagonally across a points system at a junction on the busy commuter line. The Dragonore under Angus' tee shirt; which he always wore in a pouch around his neck, suddenly started to feel warm against his skin.

"Georgina, check your Dragonore!" he whispered loudly, trying not to wake the vicar nor startle the other passengers. She touched her brooch with the Dragonore eye and smiled at Angus and they both craned forward to look out of the window. They were crossing the bridge on the approach to Blackfriars Station, and both caught sight of a fabulous silver dragon statue standing on the bridge next to the track.

"Do you think a dragon could really live in the middle of London?" asked Georgina.

"I guess so..." Angus looked at the congested traffic and the bustling streets, "but it doesn't look like the kind of place a dragon would choose to hibernate" he replied.

Hugh Penfold opened his eyes and he wiped his mouth with the back of his hand in case he had been dribbling in his sleep.

"Ah that's the boundary dragons..." he said, pretending he had not been sleeping at all, "and they mark the square mile perimeter of The City of London! My, it feels good to just rest one's eyes."

"How many are there?" asked Angus eagerly.

"Well now I'm not sure but they've been around the perimeter of the old capital for many years" he explained to the young protectors. "That one you've just seen is the Blackfriars dragon and if my

memory serves me correctly there are two on the south side of London Bridge, and some more along the Victoria Embankment of the river…" Georgina looked at Angus and smiled. She was used to her father's methodical rambling but she knew her friend would be keen to hear the locations a lot quicker. "Oh yes and there's a fabulous dragon statue in the middle of the road at Temple Bar…"

"Have you ever checked them out before?" asked Angus quickly.

"Well no… but I haven't been to London since I've been a Dragon Protector" replied the vicar thoughtfully.

"Perhaps we can get a better look at them on foot" added Georgina as the train pulled into Blackfriars station.

"Tell you what" said the Vicar, folding his newspaper and stowing it in his battered briefcase, "why don't you two go off looking for dragons and meet me for lunch at St Paul's Cathedral after my meeting… have you got a map Georgina?" In reply, she waved a pocket guidebook containing a map of the capital as the other occupants of the carriage were reaching over each other to try to retrieve their belongings from the overhead racks; and apologising to everyone as they invaded each others personal space. They left the train carriage and stepped down onto the platform to be greeted by an overwhelming smell of brake fluid. The loud banging of train doors and flapping of pigeon wings signalled their arrival into the busy London terminus.

"You might want to look out for the church of St Mary le Bow as there is supposed to be a fine dragon statue on top of that one" called the vicar to their retreating backs as he made his way out of the railway station.

Angus and Georgina checked the map and they soon had a route planned that would allow them to see as many of the statues as possible. They decided to take the Underground and head for Monument station first and this pleased Angus as he loved this mode of travel. It was only a couple of stops along the line but he intended to savour the experience and as they took the escalator down to the Underground platform he could already smell the distinctive musty smell of the tunnels. The pair talked animatedly about what they potentially might find but when they walked onto the platform Angus stopped to look around him. The platform was lit with florescent lighting that gave it that familiar half lit underground feel. The tracks, sleepers and surrounding stones were covered in black oily dirt and he could see many electrical cables running along the small wall just under the opposite platform. In this particular station

the central part of the ceiling between the two tracks was open to the outside, but the drab winter sun did not add much light to the subway. The grey platform had a yellow line near the edge which passengers were advised not to cross and a white line to mark the edge of the platform with the words 'MIND THE GAP' painted there in warning, as the train never quite met the edge of the platform.

"Look out for the sooty mice running along the sleepers" he said to Georgina.
She squealed when she spotted a few scuttling along the tracks and he assured her they would disappear when the lines started to vibrate heralding the imminent arrival of a train. The

tunnel walls were covered with cream coloured tiles that could barely be seen under all the posters and advertisements that covered it. The crowded platform was also filled with many people of all shapes, sizes and colours, and in here Angus felt you could mingle with people from anywhere in the world and that was the thing he loved best about London's Underground.

The noise of the tannoy system drew the lad's attention from studying the assembling crowd of passengers. It was difficult to understand exactly what was said as it sounded like the person speaking was holding their nose.

"Did you understand any of that?" laughed Georgina.

"Not really but I think a train is coming" replied Angus holding his nose in imitation of the announcer.

Both of them giggled as they continued to speak in that manner but stopped when they heard a faint squealing noise from the dark tunnel. Angus watched intently for the headlights of the train and could hear the drone of the engine getting louder as it got nearer. A rush of stale cold air bathed his face as the speeding train pushed the air ahead of it and out from the tunnel. Angus could smell the mustiness of the damp tunnel atmosphere as the train burst into the station; the cold air billowing jackets, trousers and skirts as it past. The train, painted bright red

colour in front, was silver grey on top and blue and white on the side with the same bright red paint on the doors. As soon as it came to a halt, the doors slid open and the passengers onboard streamed out, minding the gap as constantly reminded by the announcer over the tannoy and snaking their way to the exit. The people on the platform quickly entered the carriages with both of the young protectors. As the train was crowded they stood just inside the doors, which slid shut and the noise of the electric motors droned into action as the train slowly began to move forward. The tunnel swallowed them up with the wheels squealing intermittently with the rattle of the tracks and they disappeared into the darkness.

Chapter 9

'Monuments and More Tourists'

Angus and Georgina followed the exodus of commuters along the narrow tunnel from Monument Station to the accompaniment of a guitar-playing busker who smiled at passers by in the hope of being compensated with a few coins for his trouble. They ascended the steep escalator and emerged into daylight, breathing in the relatively fresh air of the street. Office workers jostled on the pavement, going about their daily business and the protectors rechecked the map to get their bearings. Fortunately they had come out of the Tube within sight of the Monument and with that as a landmark to guide them they could hardly go wrong. Excited to be in the historic capital of England they first walked on to London Bridge itself so they could take in the sights of the River Thames. Angus and Georgina were bustled across the wide and busy pavement as, shoulder to shoulder; they bumped and dodged through the throng of pedestrians and commuters in the buzzing financial hub of England. Red buses and black taxi cabs drove through the streets and traversed the bridge. Angus laughed at the odd sight of cyclists in pinstripe suits with

bicycle clips round their trousers to ensure they did not get caught up in the chain.

After much dodging and weaving they finally came to the middle of London Bridge. They were on the down stream side of the bridge and looking across the grey river they saw, the warship, HMS Belfast in its permanent mooring with Tower Bridge in the background. The four pointed peaks of The Tower of London were just visible behind the many buildings and trees that now surrounded it. On the other side of the river they could see the twin towers of Blackfriars station where they had just come from, with St Paul's Cathedral's famous dome just behind. The River Thames teamed with as much life as the city streets did and Angus watched boats and barges of all shapes and sizes flow up and down the city waterway.

Georgina spotted one of the boundary dragon statues outside a large pinkish coloured modern office building with what appeared to be a big chunk cut out of the architecture. They ran across the rest of the bridge to the other side of the river past a group of Japanese tourists taking pictures of each other against the river backdrop.

"Hurry Angus!" shouted Georgina excitedly. "This is a wonderful place for a dragon to hide!"

The lad was amused as the tourists began to stare and point at the crazy English girl jumping up and down in front of a silver dragon statue and they started to take pictures of her!

"You do realise you're being watched?" he said, smirking.

When she realised she was the centre of attention, Georgina's face went bright red with embarrassment and she hid behind the boundary dragon statue.

"Why didn't you tell me sooner" she whispered to him crossly.

"I tried but you weren't listening!" laughed Angus.

She refused to move while the tourists remained and only came out of hiding after they lost interest and walked off.

Angus pulled the string from around his neck, revealing the small bag he kept safe under his clothes. He opened it up and tipped out the most precious thing he owned into his hand.

"The Dragonore's cold..." he said glumly, "No

dragon here then."
Georgina was disappointed not to discover any dragon life inside the statue, and she noticed they were getting rather strange looks from a newspaper seller. He had been lucky enough to get a kiosk on the prime site of London Bridge and it allowed him to catch all the commuters and tourists, but he did see some weird things during the course of the day.

They retraced their steps and turned right off the city side of the bridge, searching the skyline for the Doric column, which was Sir Christopher Wren's monument to the Great Fire of London, simply known as 'The Monument'.

"It should be just about here…" said Angus as they turned the corner.
And there it stood, dwarfed by twentieth century office blocks. As they approached the column they realised that it was much larger than it looked before.

"Whoa… how cool is that!" said Angus once they had reached the base and admired the enormous decorated plinth. Both of them stood, heads craned backwards as they looked towards the top of the column.

"Wish we could go up there" said Georgina enthusiastically.

"We can always come back with some dragons and fly to the top if you don't fancy the 311 steps to the top!" replied

Angus smiling at her after reading the numbers from the plaque in front of them.

Georgina laughed, suddenly not feeling so keen, and then remembered something from her history lessons at school.

"The Great Fire of London started in a bakers shop in Pudding Lane" she said looking at the large plaque on the monuments wide stone base.

"Yeah, I remember that too" replied Angus as he looked at the carvings on the stone above.

"I think it rampaged all the way to Giltspur Street in Smithfield…" she continued, "I remember something about another smaller statue there… The golden boy of Pye Corner!" She waited for Angus to acknowledge what she had told him and was just about to tell him off for not listening when she realised they were being watched. It was the same tourists from before and as some waved to her one or two jumped up and down imitating her earlier antics. She could feel her face flushing with embarrassment again so she turned away from them and moved closer to Angus.

"What are you looking at?" she asked, hoping the tourists would get bored soon and move on.

The lad was studying the intricate stonework above the plaque and they both set to work analysing what appeared to be an interesting story told in pictures on the relief carvings around the plinth. They did not have much luck interpreting them until Georgina realised that a nearby information board explained everything about the newly restored carvings and their meanings. Soon she had found an allegorical figure of the City of London with another figure representing Time behind it and two goddesses representing Plenty and Peace. At the feet of the figures was a beehive signifying industry and underneath that was a dragon supporting a shield bearing the arms of the City of London amidst the ruins of the Great Fire. Something occurred to Georgina as she looked at that part closely, but she said nothing and decided to keep it for another time.

"No one here either then" said Georgina finally breaking the silence.

But Angus was busy reading about The Great Fire, which destroyed over 13,000 houses as well as countless other important buildings back in 1666.

"You know..." he replied finally, "the one good thing to come out of the fire was that it brought an end to the Plague."

"Yeah I suppose you're right, but I wonder if it was really an accident" said Georgina mysteriously.

"What do you mean?"

"Oh nothing… Just a thought… never mind" she replied, "Come on, let's go somewhere else" she finished hastily checking to see if the tourists had moved on.
Both protectors were disappointed not to find a dragon hiding in this famous landmark and it seemed strange that no dragons were benefiting from such wonderful places to hide.

Consulting the map again they headed up King William Street through the heart of the City. The street buzzed with the sound of people and traffic as they went about their daily business. Just like New York the whole city seemed alive and in constant motion. It was a chilly crisp day and the sun made best efforts to brighten up the winter. Angus chatted to Georgina about general things but neither of them dared speak about the lost eggs not wishing to dampen the mood of the day. Red London buses lined the road, dropping off and picking up passengers as taxis, delivery vans and many other vehicles passed by in endless procession. The roadways of the vast city were its arteries through which flowed its life blood. After about ten minutes of walking the pair reached a large road junction and found many marvellous dragon statues on each corner. This was Threadneedle Street where the Stock Exchange and the Bank of England were situated and Angus thought that

Macklin would certainly have approved of these surroundings for a worthy hiding place. The regal looking historic buildings with their majestic stone facades dominated the corner sites.

"Let's check these statues out then" said Angus pointing to one that stood in front of the Exchange and had many other statues beside it.

It was obvious from the lack of warmth in their Dragonore there were no dragons present there either, not even a trace.

"All these statues and no dragons… It just seems such a waste" said Georgina dejectedly.

"Surely there must be some dragons in this City" said Georgina, "we did detect one from the train… perhaps we were mistaken or they have heard about the hunt for Rhys' eggs and are out searching…"

"I don't think so, we don't have any awakened dragons logged in the City yet" he replied honestly, and then seeing her sad look added, "let's not give up though. Can I have a look at that guidebook of yours again?"

Angus studied the simplified map and the key at the back of the guidebook with the positions of the boundary dragons clearly marked on the streets.

"Mmmm… if we walk up Cheapside now and try to find the church your dad was talking about…"

"Oh yes..." added Georgina brightening up, "then we can meet Daddy for lunch!"

Angus folded the guidebook and they turned to go but Georgina stopped in her tracks, her face suddenly stern and serious.

"What is it?" asked Angus concerned, "What's the matter?"

"They're following us!" she cried, "I'm sure of it!"

He looked in the same direction and saw a maroon tour bus passing by with some people on the top waving at them and taking pictures. It was the same tourists from the bridge and Angus laughed as one or two of them jumped up and down whilst pointing at his friend. He turned smiling to comment to Georgina and thought better of it when he saw the scowl on her face.

Above the sounds of the traffic and the occasional siren, church bells rang out, so they knew that they were close. The bells were announcing the impending hour of eleven o'clock just as the pair turned into a small alleyway known as Bow Lane. These were the famous Bow Bells and anyone born within hearing distance of this melodious sound was said to be a true Londoner; a Cockney. The pair soon spied what they had hoped to find, a stunning dragon perched on a golden orb

on the very top of the tall spire of another Christopher Wren built church.

"Well he was a busy man..." said Angus sarcastically, after Georgina had told him who the architect was.
He saw brightness in her brooch coming from the gem in the eye of the dragon. At last the Dragonore glowed and Angus squinted closer to the golden statue above; 'At last!'

Chapter 10

'Snubbed Before Lunch'

The statue showed no sign of movement and as they were rather conspicuous standing in the middle of a busy street Angus was reluctant to start shouting up at the golden figure.

"Let's move round here" he suggested, pointing to the right hand side of the tower.

Now that they were out of the sight of passers by Angus tried to coax the dragon out of its hiding place. It soon became apparent that his usual tactic was not going to work.

"We are members of the SSDP… can you come down and speak to us please?" added Georgina trying to help.

Nothing happened and Angus wondered what they would have to do to get the unwilling inhabitant of the spire to reveal itself. Angus was predictably getting impatient and decided to try another tack.

"We need your help… Please come down!" he shouted holding up his Dragonore as it glowed brightly.

At first nothing happened but then Angus began to notice the statue blurring at the edges which was a sure sign that a dragon was about to morph.

"Did you see that?" cried Georgina excitedly.

The dragon had moved its head to look down at them and their search and belief was justified as a morphing figure floated down to the ground in front of them.

The bronze dragon was very wary of the pair and shifted uneasily on its feet, looking furtively around as if expecting an ambush. The dragon was smaller than Pyrra and although that could allow you to think it was female Angus knew from the shape of the head it was male.

"Hi..." said Georgina enthusiastically, causing the dragon to jump, "Oh sorry..." she added more quietly, "I'm Georgina and this is Angus. What's your name?"

The dragon did not answer and just stood blinking at them causing Angus to think maybe he did not speak English. The young protectors looked at each other wondering what to do next.

"My... name... is..." replied the dragon slowly as if saying the words for the first time, but he failed to finish the sentence and began to scan the skies again with a nervous expression. Both of them were so stunned by the weird manner of this dragon that they did not react; the dragon suddenly said.

"You… have… Dragonore?"

Angus realised that the dragon had been drawn down by the Dragonore they bore; dragons being naturally inquisitive creatures.

"Yes we're members of The Secret Society of Dragon Protectors" replied Angus also keeping his voice gentle.

"No… can't be… Society all gone!" replied the dragon who was very wary indeed and kept shifting about, hopping from foot to foot.

"No the SSDP is back and we have many protectors keeping an eye on loads of awakened…"

Angus stopped talking as he noticed that the dragon was not looking very happy.

"Are you okay?" asked Georgina with concern. "You look scared."

The small dragon was very agitated and not willing to speak to them. What was really strange was he did not seem worried about people in the street being able to see him, but he did appear to be worried about something coming from the sky. He constantly scanned the rooftops and sky nervously; flicking his yellow eyes from one spot to another.

"Do not speak… to strangers!" replied the dragon, but he was looking at the ground and shaking his head.

Angus was finding the whole conversation very frustrating and wondered if this new found dragon was suffering from a memory disorder from the Hibernation.

"But we're friends, why can't you speak to us? We won't harm you!" asked Georgina slightly hurt.

The nervous dragon eyed them distrustfully and looked to the sky again.

"Can't… must stay on watch… need to go now!" whispered the dragon before flying back up to the top of the spire and morphing into the ornamental statue again.

Both protectors stood stunned by this bizarre behaviour. They looked up at the statue as if expecting the dragon to come back telling them it was all a big joke; both wore the same bemused expression.

"That was very strange!" said Angus beginning to laugh.

"We didn't even get that one's name… you must be losing your touch!" smiled Georgina. "Come on, we don't have much time before we meet Daddy for lunch but if we hurry we can maybe check out another statue."

"Which one do you want to see" asked Angus looking at the map?

"Well... if we continue along Cheapside we can pass the dragon statue at Goldsmiths Hall then we can just cut down the next street and end up at St Paul's" she replied as she pointed to the map.

It turned out that the statue was a lot closer than they thought and after finding nothing there, they continued on their way to the lunch rendezvous at St Paul's. Angus was bemused by the morning's events and somewhat disappointed by their lack of findings. Not much to report back to Rathlin at the SSDP headquarters except for a rather reluctant and extremely nervous dragon at St Mary le Bow.

"I guess we might as well" said Angus glumly.

What started out as a promising dragon finding adventure was turning out to be very disappointing, 'Still' thought Angus, 'At least I got to spend some time with Georgina'. Georgina had already started to walk on and just as Angus went to follow he heard a car accelerating hard and turned to see a small red sports car zoom down Cheapside in the direction they were heading. It sped past and without any hesitation skidded left at the junction without even stopping at the 'give way' sign. Angus could imagine what his Dad would have to say about that kind of driving and he just shook his head and hurried

after Georgina who had now stopped at the corner.

"You forget how massive the Cathedral is until you see it close up!" said Georgina as he reached her.

Angus did not reply as his attention was drawn along the road to the same red sports car he had just seen moments before. The car had swerved across the street and was now parked haphazardly in front of a big Victorian building. The driver was obviously in a hurry and did not care that a delivery truck and motorbike messenger had no choice but to screech to a halt behind the sports car as they could not get past in the narrow street. The building was mainly used by large international companies in this financial area of the City and Angus noticed the name 'Halcyon House' over the door as they crossed the street towards the cathedral. He could see it was a woman driving the car as she tapped an impatient rhythm on the steering wheel, but her head was hidden from view as the car was too low. A man in a light grey uniform hurried out from beneath a grey stone arch in the majestic looking building. He opened the car door and the woman got out just as the van and the motorbike finally managed to squeeze past the obstructive sports car. The irritated woman barked instructions into her mobile phone as she glanced over her shoulder at a four wheel drive with blacked out windows. Angus realised it had been waiting for the van to move to enable it to pull up close behind the car. As he and Georgina walked along the street Angus tried to keep track of her as she wittered about the cathedral whilst he attempted to keep an eye on the drama across the street. Both proved difficult since Georgina was in full flow and the buses and cars made it virtually impossible to see all that was taking place. He could just make out the woman as she strode purposefully up the front steps of the building and tossed her car keys to a man who caught them deftly. As she disappeared through the main door of the building, two surly men in dark suits exited the four-wheel drive glancing furtively around them. They walked to the back of the vehicle and lifted two identical boxes from inside before quickly walking inside the building in the wake of the impatient woman. The man who had caught the car keys with great dexterity got into the drivers seat of the sports car and drove off presumably to park the car somewhere less obstructive to traffic. The driver of the black four by four followed and in a matter of seconds the commotion was over and the street returned to normal.

Angus studied the building and could see the arched architecture repeated along the ground level with large multi paned windows covering the entire building for about eight floors. What made

this building very unusual was the way it curved with the road as the street bent its way around the eastern end of St Paul's. During all this time Georgina had been talking and after complaining out loud that her tummy was rumbling she remembered something else to tell Angus.

"Oh yes, I wanted to talk to you about something I saw on the base of the Monument..." said the girl.

She realised she was talking to herself and spun round to see Angus stood stock still on the pavement some fifty yards behind. Suddenly he seemed to jerk as if he had just woken from a trance, and turning he ran to catch her up. He sprinted the distance so that fast he could barely speak once he reached her, however she noticed this was not through exertion, but through excitement.

"You haven't heard a word I've been saying, have you..."

"Sor...ry... want to..." panted Angus.

"Not sorry, it'll just have to wait for now as we are late for Daddy... and he so dislikes unpunctuality" she said a little haughtily, tossing her hair to emphasise the point.

Georgina glanced around to look in the direction she had been walking and started to wave.

"There he is! DADDY!" she squealed as the vicar came from the far side of St Paul's beneath its world famous dome.

"But…" tried Angus again.

Georgina hated being late for anything and was not going to be this time either. She grabbed Angus' elbow and steered him all the way to the meeting place on the steps of Christopher Wrens Cathedral, the jolly vicar was waving frantically now he had caught sight of them.

"Ah there you are… hungry are we?" Hugh called as they reached him.

Angus had given up trying to tell Georgina what he was so desperate to say before and now began to doubt his own mind as to what he thought he had seen.

"Just in time for lunch then… I want to take you to this marvellous eatery… best fish and chips in London, what do you say eh?"

Angus' mind raced. He needed to get his thoughts in order, and he had made a mental note of the building name and what street it was in. He could not really get his head around his discovery, but he also needed to eat. It seemed sensible to tell the story once to both of the Penfolds. At least, when he could get a chance to speak that was!

They descended a flight of brick steps into what was once a cellar and Georgina wrinkled her nose at the smell of damp, lingering in the air. Empty bottles and flagons covered with cobwebs lined the walls, looking as if they had a story of their own to tell. The trio sat at a round table on hard upright chairs in the sawdust-strewn cellar of Muddefords. Angus played idly with the saltcellar as Georgina's father ordered fish and chips all round.

"My dear boy you look as if you've seen a ghost! Are you all right lad? You don't look quite the ticket" asked the vicar concerned.

Angus looked up and thought, 'Here goes!'

"I've just seen Meredith and two of her men were carrying the eggs into a building" he replied quietly.

Chapter 11

'Stop the Bus'

Now he had their full attention! Georgina stared at him open mouthed, the straw from her lemonade bobbing in the glass where she had let go of it suddenly. Hugh Penfold was the first to speak and he laughed in a hearty fashion trying to break the sudden seriousness of the atmosphere.

"Now when did you see this?"

"About half an hour ago, just before we met you" replied Angus.

"But why didn't you say anything before" asked Georgina in surprise?

"I… wasn't sure… in fact, I'm still not sure" replied the young protector.

"Ah here's the food! Why don't you tell us exactly what you saw…" said the vicar, smiling at his dinner,

Angus waited for the waiter to finish placing the heavily laden white plates onto the table before he started to recall what he saw. He tried to account for everything as he saw it and not change anything or embellish it in any way.

"So if you didn't see her face what makes you

think it was Meredith?" asked Georgina.

Angus thought about this and why he was so sure it was her, but he could not put it into words.

"I can't explain it…" he answered lamely.

"So you didn't actually see the eggs, just two plain boxes?" asked the vicar before stuffing another large forkful of chips into his mouth.

He thought about the answers to their questions and began to doubt his theory.

"Yes, but they were about the right size…" he knew how silly that sounded and stopped.

"I know you're anxious to restore the eggs to Rhys lad, but I think your overactive imagination is running away with you" said the Vicar kindly.

The more the Penfolds questioned Angus, the more he began to doubt what he had seen and he ended up disproving his own theory. After all it did seem rather ridiculous that he would come to London and be on that street at the particular moment that Meredith was unloading the stolen eggs. He was so desperate to find the eggs he was beginning to see things that were not there and it could have been anything in those boxes!

"Yeah… you're probably right… I'm just being stupid… Meredith told me to my face she wouldn't touch the eggs!"

Georgina watched him carefully and smiled when he shrugged and grinned back at her. He tucked into his fish and chips, which were exceptionally good and put any thought of Meredith and the eggs from his mind. Well, at least for now!

A few minutes later the vicar wiped crumbs from the side of his mouth with a paper serviette, smacked his lips and pushed his empty plate away.

"Didn't I tell you they were the best fish and chips in town…" he beamed, "Now then I need to visit my solicitor in Chancery Lane so you two can go off and find that dragon statue at Temple Bar if you like… did you see any hidden dragons in your wanderings?"

"Yes we did!" answered Georgina as Angus was still eating.

"REALLY!" exclaimed the vicar rather too loudly, "Well how exciting, do tell."

Georgina flushed red as people at other tables stared at them.

"Not much to tell really…" she replied quietly hoping her father lower his tone, "we couldn't find any dragons in the statues until the one at St Mary le Bow and that one didn't seem very friendly" she explained.

"He was just a bit weird… as if he was looking out for something!" said Angus through his final mouthful of chips, all thoughts of Meredith forgotten.

"Well that's a pity, still I'm sure Rathlin will be keen to hear about him and maybe he'll have better luck than you did" said Hugh before he drank the last of his cola and wiped his face with a napkin. "If you've found one dragon then I would assume you might be able to find at least one more."

"I guess..." replied Georgina, "but it does seem a bit pointless when they won't even speak to you when we do find them... this one was very rude!"

"I'm sure there is a perfectly simple explanation for his behaviour... I'll be off now and finished by five..." he said standing up and folding his napkin, "Now remember I'll meet you at the National History Museum, Exhibition Road entrance and we'll go and see the dinosaurs... Toodlepip!" he called as he bumbled off in the direction of the door clutching his battered old briefcase.

"Bye Daddy, thanks for lunch!" Georgina called affectionately after him.

Angus gave the vicar a wave as well before turning to Georgina and mimicking her farewell. She laughed and slapped his arm playfully telling him to be quiet.

"Let's go and find this Temple Bar dragon statue then" said Angus feigning hurt and rubbing his arm.

Georgina produced the guidebook again.

"According to this it should be right here where Fleet Street joins The Strand" she said pointing into the page. "You know I always think of those streets being red!" she laughed. Georgina was thinking about the Monopoly board game and wondered why these two particular streets were included on the original version.

They made for the exit and out into the street where Georgina stood looking confused.

"It's this way" said Angus confidently.

"Are you sure?" she asked looking at the map and turning it sideways.

"Trust me" he grinned.

It was not long before he was proved correct as they quickly found St Paul's again and began to walk along the south side of the great Cathedral. Soon the sign for Fleet Street appeared and, knowing it was a long road Georgina had a better idea.

"Let's take the bus!" she said impetuously as one passed by.

Angus nodded his agreement and they made for a nearby bus stop to wait for the next famous London red double-decker.

Within a minute or so a bus appeared with at

least another three or four behind it. Georgina checked that it would indeed pass Temple Bar as they showed the driver their travel cards. As the doors swooshed shut behind them, the bus pulled away and the pair quickly climbed the steep curved stairs in a race to get to the upper deck. The movement of the bus rocked them from side to side and they hung onto the rail, Georgina giggling like anything. They noticed the front seat was empty and they both collapsed into it just as the bus began to accelerate again. Both were glad of the respite from walking.

The top of the bus swayed slowly as the driver manoeuvred down the cambered street. Years of road works had seen the grey tarmac dug up and resurfaced many times making it bumpy and uneven. The bus never got up to any great speed as the traffic was busy and it had to stop at every bus stop. The two young dragon protectors were glued to the window, eagerly taking in every detail around them. The pavements swarmed with people going about their business as the cars dodged and weaved past delivery vans, taxis and buses. When they reached a main junction the lights turned to red and the bus driver broke hard to avoid going through. Both of them had to grab the silver bar in front of the large glass window to avoid being thrown into it.

"Sorry folks" shouted the driver to everyone on the bus his

thick Cockney accent plain for all to hear.
The junction swarmed with cars moving in the other direction and turning into the other street as pedestrians walked quickly across the road at the signal of the green man. From the position Angus sat in, the pedestrians looked like they were dancing, as their movement had a kind of rhythm to it. The bus began to move off again at the invitation of the green light and after a few more stops they could not miss the dragon, standing tall and proud, in the middle of the street. Georgina read from the guidebook-come-map they had been using and told Angus that the Temple Bar area was an ancient gateway to the City of London. The western most boundary on the road to Westminster and was originally put there to regulate trade.

"The word 'Bar' literally means 'barrier' which linked the trading part of the City to Parliament" she added as they rang the bell and got off at the next stop.
Angus led the way to the statue and looked at the large towering plinth on top of which perched a majestic black dragon.

"Whoa it's so cool" he exclaimed, impressed.

"It's copied straight from the City's coat of arms... Look" said Georgina holding up the front cover of the guidebook for him to see.

There could be little doubt in the mind of anyone who saw this

statue that it had been strategically placed in front of the Royal Courts of Justice for a reason. The significance of the position would leave any dragon feeling extremely important.

They crossed the road excited at the prospect of possibly finding a dragon there, but making sure they were safe from the traffic. The pedestal that gave the dragon such a lofty position was carved and worked with a variety of details which included a statue of a woman. As they approached Angus felt his Dragonore warming slightly through the pouch on his chest and he quickly looked at Georgina and saw the eye of her brooch glimmer.

Chapter 12

'The Light is on but Nobody's Home'

Surely they had found another dragon! Angus looked up at the black statue with its proud stance, holding a shield in its fore claws. The chest was thrust forward and the wings spread wide from the scaly body. Angus made an attempt to greet any potential dragon that might possibly be concealed there, but if there was a dragon hiding in the shape, it stayed steely silent within the cold metal statue.

"It seems as if a dragon is here… at least according to the Dragonore" said Angus.

"Maybe there is, but it looks as if he is just as unfriendly as the one at the church" suggested Georgina.

Angus thought he saw some movement in the statue and stared intently at it, hoping to catch some indication of life, but nothing happened.

"Maybe I was mistaken… or there's no-one at home" he said, remembering a similar experience whilst searching for Cyru last summer.

"Why don't we search for some more elsewhere" suggested Georgina.

They started to walk away and Angus turned to have one last

look and there it was again! Now he was sure the statue moved or at least the morphed shape of a dragon inside it had.

"What's the matter?" asked Georgina.

"Nothing… I just thought…" he replied, then shaking his head, "C'mon let's go" he finished, turning his back on something he was struggling to figure out.

The young protector knew when something was not quite right and whatever it was he was definitely going to get to the bottom of it.

"There are supposed to be more dragon statues at Smithfield… just a short walk… are you up for that?" he said.

"My feet are killing me" said Georgina smiling through gritted teeth, and not wishing to dampen her friend's enthusiasm, "But yes, it seems silly not to since we are here now."

She wished wholeheartedly she had not worn her new boots, which Angus had not noticed anyway.

"What's at Smithfield?" she asked brightly.

Angus took the guidebook and read aloud the bit he had glanced at earlier.

"The Smithfield area of London has a long and colourful history. Livestock traders for the last 900 years used to meet on this green plain just outside of the City Wall to sell animals, which they literally walked to market from all over Britain. Nowadays, Smithfield is the largest meat market in the country, but it used to witness even bloodier activities…" he recited, "Before Tyburn became the popular place for public executions in London, this was the grisly location. Famous Smithfield executions include William Wallace, the leader of the Scots in their wars of independence, executed in 1305, and Wat Tyler, the leader of the Peasants Revolt of 1381. This once grassy field had also been the scene of jousting and other large public gatherings, just beyond the City wall..." he continued.

Georgina had by now lost interest and began stuffing a folded tissue into the heel of her boot to try to stop it rubbing.

"What's up?" asked Angus noticing she had stopped listening.

"Just trying to stop my heel hurting!" she replied.

"Oh yeah… new boots…nice!" said Angus.

Georgina brightened a little, 'At last he noticed, maybe it was almost worth it' she thought.

"So what do you think?" asked Angus.

"Of what?" asked Georgina in reply, still fixing her boots.

"Of going to Smithfield!" replied Angus.

Georgina looked up at him and screwed up her face.

"It's a bit gruesome isn't it… and what's there that we would want to see?" she replied.

"Oh c'mon it's cool and they have some superb statues on the building… look" he said holding open the page with a picture of the market.
Georgina nodded her agreement but insisted they got another bus, which Angus did not mind doing anyway.

Twenty minutes later they were standing in front of an enormous covered market, but being mid afternoon there was not much activity. Trading was done in the early hours of the morning and concluded by the time most postal or office workers descended on that area of London. Only the recently hosed down pavements gave a clue to that early morning's brisk trade where wholesalers and butchers came from all over the country to buy their meat for their customers fresh from Smithfield Market. But such was the fastidiousness of the market cleaners you could not even guess what went on there. They walked throughout the market area looking for any dragon statues that might prove to be a hiding place for a dragon. They had already come across another boundary dragon and found no sign of life but Angus was hopeful when he saw the outside of the main building.

"Wow, check those two out!" he shouted, spotting the

identical pair of silver dragons peering down from the external façade of the building. "I reckon a meat market is a very cool place for a dragon to live... Pyrra wouldn't like it though... she prefers her food warm!" he added sharing the joke with Georgina.

She grimaced at the thought of what he said and she did not really want to know what dragons ate or how. She walked on into the space underneath the central archway called Grand Avenue, punctuated by a row of bright red telephone boxes. She stopped under the big glass roof to try to fix her boot again.

"You don't see many of those any more" said Georgina glancing up at the telephone boxes as she eased her blistered heel back into her boot.

Angus noticed that the eye of her dragon brooch glistened in the gloomy interior and he looked up at the arches of the great market place.

"Something's here!" he shouted indicating her Dragonore. They walked a little further and suddenly, in the middle of Smithfield Market, Angus' Dragonore glowed with such intensity he had to grab the pouch and hold it away from his skin for fear of burning. Georgina thought her brooch would explode and looking up in the riveted steel rafters of the covered meat market they saw, not just one, but a whole bunch of dragons. Angus could only wish that Pyrra was with him to witness this spectacle.

Chapter 13

'The City Guardians'

It was difficult to count exactly how many dragons there were, but he could see all shapes and sizes. The inhabitants of the rafters were too busy arguing to notice the two young protectors and had their backs to them so Angus and Georgina unashamedly listened in to their conversation. Angus motioned Georgina to be quiet and she followed him over to a gap in the brightly coloured railings that lined the inside of the market. The two protectors did not really want to eavesdrop, but they also did not want to scare the dragons off after working so hard to find them. The conversation started to become clearer and to their surprise, they appeared to be the main topic.

"The humans had Dragonore and spoke of the Secret Society of Dragon Protectors" said one of the dragons.

"Who told you this?" snarled a gruff voice that reminded Angus of another dragon.

"Fulbert..." was the meek reply.

"And how could Fulbert speak to them when he was on duty?" growled the gruff voice.

"He swears he never stopped watching Faris, he only spoke to them briefly to tell them to leave..." replied the meek voiced dragon.

"He should not have spoken to them at all, they are imposters and the SSDP does not exist!" bellowed the dragon called Faris.

When they heard that last statement Angus started to move forward, but Georgina wisely grabbed his arm and silently implored him to stay hidden.

"What else did they want?" asked Faris.

"Fulbert said they had discovered many dragons and that the Society protected them" replied the meek dragon.

"Now Lyell, we all know that Fulbert hit his head very hard that night he fell from his tower while asleep. He struggles to follow what is going on around him sometimes and that is why I keep him on guard duty so much… it's the safest place for him… but all this talk of many dragons being found, well it's nonsense" said Faris calmly, "If that was the case we would have seen some sign of them by now. We are the last of our kind and we must stick together no matter what!"

The dragons roared their approval of his words and Angus wondered how they were ever going to persuade them of the truth.

"I think we should leave now and come back with Pyrra and Wymarc" he whispered.

"I agree… we definitely could use some reinforcements" she replied just as quietly.

They both began to step slowly back the way they came when Angus spotted another dragon flying in through the large opening to the market. The dragon was green, but not the same shade as Pyrra, and had a mottling of brown on his underside. The new dragon deftly flicked his wings wide and tilted them just at the correct angle to allow him to take his place next to the others.

"Ah Wulfric glad you could make it!" said Faris.

"My apologies Faris… by the way who are the two humans watching us from below?"

Suddenly all conversation stopped as the dragons turned towards the intruders. Many different coloured dragon eyes glared in the direction of the two companions; all reflecting a conflicting mixture of mistrust and curiosity.

"I don't know who you are or what you want, but we don't need you or your protection" growled one of the dragons.

Angus walked forward, his courage, as always, arrived quickly, despite being faced by so many hostile dragons.

"We're sorry to intrude but we're from the SSDP…"

"The Society ended hundreds of years ago. We've had not contact since long before the Great Fire and we don't need the help of any humans" interrupted Faris.

"But we can show you if you just give us a chance… Rathlin Tek will be able to explain…" chimed in Georgina.

"And who is Rathlin Tek?" asked Faris again as he dropped to the ground in front of them.

The appearance of the black dragon was a shock to Angus. It was like seeing a ghost. Despite this, he answered boldly.

"He's the leader of the SSDP. The Teks have been watching over dragons for hundreds of years during the Great Hibernation".

Faris stared into Angus' eyes as if trying to penetrate the boy's thoughts or detect any sign of untruthfulness, but the lad just met the dragon's gaze with the same intensity. The large black dragon was impressed with this young human's courage, but did not want any interference from mankind.

"What business do you have here anyway?" asked Wulfric as he too dropped to the ground just behind Faris.

"Well as we've been trying to tell you, we are here from The Secret Society of Dragon Protectors, tracking and monitoring all dragons as they awaken from the Great Hibernation…"

"You seem to think we should be grateful to see you. Well we are the City Guardians and we have no need of human protection... In fact *WE* protect *YOU*!" interrupted Faris again.

"Well how rude!" said Georgina loudly and she sat down hard on the curbside despite the dampness, kicked off her boot and started to rub her sore foot, muttering angrily under her breath.

"If I were you I'd go back to your boss and tell him you found no dragons in London. Humans and dragons don't mix too well and we certainly do not want you here!" said Faris gruffly.

There was general muttering from the other dragons still hiding in the rafters. Georgina was dreadfully unhappy with the behavior of these dragons and her sore feet, blistered from all the walking they had done, were not helping her mood.

"Doesn't he remind you of someone?" she hissed from the ground.

Angus had been thinking the same ever since he had first heard Faris speak and the black dragon's resemblance was uncanny. In fact if it were not for his green eyes and the fact that the dragon was dead, Angus would have thought it was his old enemy stood before him.

"Yeah, Felspar" he muttered not taking his eyes from the leader of the City Dragons.

The large black dragon bridled at the mention of Felspar's name. In fact Angus could see that the mere mention of his name had greatly incensed the large dragon.

"So you know Felspar do you?" spat Wulfric.

The young protectors realised the mood of the dragons had changed and Angus felt as afraid now as he had been at his last encounter with Felspar.

"That vicious and vindictive low life who brought shame on our kind..." snarled Wulfric as Faris turned his back on the pair in contempt, at once mistaking their relationship with the evil dragon. Angus tried to explain.

"No... you don't understand... I k..."

"ENOUGH!" bellowed the black dragon. "Leave us alone and never come back or the next time we will be more than angry!"

That said Faris, who was presumably the leader, unfurled his wings and turned to the other dragons.

"None of you are to have anything to do with these humans, is that clear? Make them leave here now!"

With a flick of his large wings he made a dramatic exit as he flew out from the covered market.

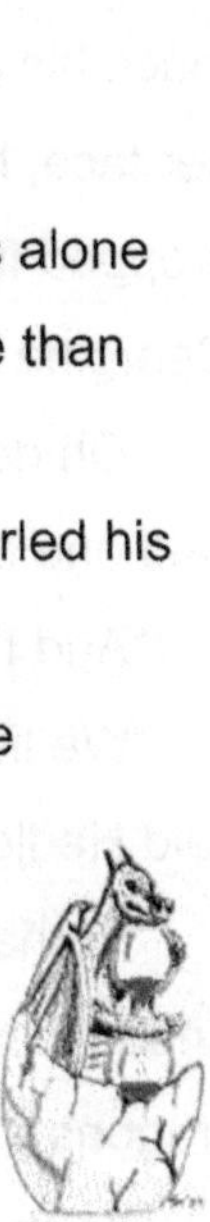

Chapter 14

'Band Aid'

Georgina replaced her boot, ignoring the pain in the face of the danger she realised they were in. She could see Angus was angry at being cut-off so abruptly and she wanted to be near him to calm him down.

"Come on Angus, this is pointless… let's go" she said quietly as she stood up, moving to his side.

The young lad turned to look at her pretty face when he felt her touch his arm. She was trembling, and seeing the concern in her face, he immediately mellowed. One or two of the dragons dropped from the rafters and landed beside the pair causing Georgina to spin her head nervously in their direction.

"Oh don't you worry about him lovey, he's full of hot air" said one of the dragon's, "My name is Hedley."

"And I'm Latimer" added the other.

"We live here on the market… in the dragons just outside" said Hedley.

"Perhaps you saw them dearie?" asked Latimer.

Angus was stunned, as he did not expect a greeting from these dragons after what their leader had just instructed.

"Yeah… they're really cool" replied Angus cautiously.

"Oh we're so happy to hear you say that dearie" gushed Latimer.

"Well we know it's not the plushest place in the world but it home and they have painted it with the sweetest colours!" added Hedley.

Angus stood open mouthed; as he had never seen dragons act this way. At least not the males anyway!

"You two had better remember what Faris told us" said Wulfric before he flew off the rafter with a grunt in the direction of the young protectors and exited the same way as Faris.

The other dragons followed, leaving the two humans alone with the rather comical pair from Smithfield Market.

"Faris had issues with Felspar and that wound is still a little raw. But don't worry lovey, he'll come round" said Hedley once the other dragons were out of sight.

Angus, his face still a picture of disbelief, looked to his female companion for some help in understanding what was going on. These two dragons spoke as if they were one; with one sentence rolling after the other so quickly it was difficult to keep up. Georgina on the other hand had completely changed her demeanor from being afraid, to absolute delight.

"I'm sure he will..." she said quickly, "How

many of you live in London and how long have you been awake and…?"

"Oh steady lovey, one question at a time… not many, only nine… and we've been awake for a long, long time" replied Hedley.

Georgina looked at Angus and then her face lit up with excitement.

"Do you have any young?" she enthused.

Hedley looked at Latimer with a blank expression and then both of them began to laugh.

"No dearie we're all boys together… not seen a female dragon for hundreds of years…" replied Latimer, "Doesn't she have beautiful hair for a human?" he said to Hedley as he gently caressed her hair, the other dragon nodding his agreement.

Georgina looked disappointed at this answer and then remembering another question she decided to take advantage of the talkative dragons they had met at last.

"Tell me something, why do the boundary dragons face outwards in their statues, away from the City?" she asked inquisitively and amused by this dragon's fascination with her long hair.

"Well lovey, what you see is just a shell, but we face

outwards so we can see enemies approaching the City from within the boundaries… you see we really are the City Guardians" replied Hedley.

"Rather ironic really as we didn't see the enemy in our midst…" added Latimer.

Angus found the way the two dragons kept talking around each other very hard to follow but he could definitely understand what they said about the enemy within. 'We know all about those' he thought to himself.

Hedley continued.

"Felspar wanted to be one of us, but he lived outside of the boundaries in East London" added Latimer.

"Faris was the elected leader of the City Guardians, but Felspar was always challenging him. There was no sense of brotherhood felt between those two" continued Hedley.

The two dragons paused as if reflecting on some tragic event that had happened in the past and both protectors sensed they were not going to hear any more about it now.

"Tell us how you survive here in the middle of the city, aren't you a bit far from your natural food source?" Georgina asked breaking them from their thoughts.

"Well it took us a while to acquire a taste for

refrigerated meat I must say..." replied Hedley.

"Gave us terrible indigestion to start with dearie..." added Latimer.

"Of course we all prefer our meat to be warm and preferably bleating, but needs must and all that" finished Hedley.

"Pyrra wouldn't like that much!" said Angus looking from one dragon to the other as he was not sure which one would speak next.

"Who is this Pyrra you speak of lovey?" asked Hedley curiously.

"She's my friend and I'm her protector!" replied Angus.

"She sounds wonderful; perhaps we'll get to meet her" said Latimer.

"Maybe, but actually we need your help!" said Angus seeing a chance to return to the reason for their visit.

"Well dearie why didn't you say so!" exclaimed Latimer slapping Angus on the back playfully.

"We'd love to help!" cried Hedley.

Georgina giggled at the look on Angus' face as he was clearly thrown by the comedic antics of these two very strange dragons. She put it down to the isolation they had experienced by being cut-off from the rest of the dragon community for such a long time.

"Yeah..." continued Angus rubbing his shoulder, "thanks!"

"The society has never found any dragons in the City before and it's fortunate that we've met you..." said Georgina buttering up the dragons some more, "you probably don't know this but the Great Hibernation has finally come to an end."

"Oh we all know about that dearie, we all saw old Barfoot in his message" threw in Latimer, matter-of-factly.

This surprised even Angus as most of the dragons had no recollection of the old Ward when he attempted to awaken them from their centuries' long slumber. Then Angus realised these dragons had not really been hibernating and therefore would not be suffering from the same kind of memory issues that the hibernating dragons had.

"I remember when he showed me to the Cor Stan and let me get my first piece of Dragonore... How is old Barfoot anyway?" asked Hedley.

The question brought back memories of the day Barfoot died in front of Angus. The old dragon had passed on the mantle of Ward to Godroi after the Trials and it was still a painful memory for the lad. He saw that Georgina was struggling not to cry and decided he had better answer.

"Ward Barfoot died during the summer…" he said sadly, "his time was at an end and he passed his powers onto Godroi after he won the Trials."

The two dragons were crestfallen at the news; both of them looked as if they had lost a close friend.

"He was a wonderful dragon dearie" said Latimer sniffing slightly.

"The best lovey" added Hedley, "Oh my, the lads'll be really upset to hear this bit of bad news!"

"I'm really sorry but it was what he wanted and if it had not been for Pyrra then Felspar would have taken his powers for himself!" continued Angus.

"Well now, just you wait 'til Faris hears this bit of news!" shouted Hedley, "I wouldn't be surprised if he doesn't go and hunt that good for nothing down and do him in himself!"

Georgina was about to tell them about Felspar and the knight George but Angus hushed her with a look that said 'not now'.

"Because the Hibernation would only lead to your downfall, the Ward told all dragons that it was time to awaken and begin building again for the future… otherwise you will all die out!" said Angus seriously.

"Oh my… well that's going to prove to be a bit difficult for us lot here in London!" laughed Latimer.

"Too right lovey!" agreed Hedley grinning broadly.

"The first dragon eggs have already been laid… the first for many centuries!" Angus paused as this news sunk in.
They two dragons were obviously impressed and curious so Angus continued.

"The problem is… well the eggs have gone missing"

"What do you mean by missing?" cried Hedley.

"I think he means nicked dearie!" replied Latimer.
"Pilfered… blagged… robbed… stolen even!"

"That's a bit careless! Some bunch of protectors you lot are!" added Hedley in derision.
Angus got the irony of the joke but it did not make him laugh.

"So I guess you don't know who done it and you would like us to help you look for them?" suggested Latimer.

"Can you keep your eyes open?" replied Angus nodding his agreement to the previous statement.

"Of course we'll keep a look out lovey… that's our job!" replied Hedley importantly.
The two young protectors smiled at the dragons in appreciation of this unexpected and very welcome turnabout.

Suddenly Georgina looked at her watch and motioned urgently to Angus.

"Angus we need to go… Daddy will be waiting for us at the Museum" she said urgently.

Georgina, who hated being late for anything, took out her Underground map and shook it open. She was a bit flustered and the dragons noticed it.

"Don't you worry about a thing lovey, we'll take you there" chimed Hedley, "I presume you can ride?"

Angus and Georgina did not hesitate in jumping on the backs of the dragons, as they knew; this was definitely the fastest way to travel.

Chapter 15

'London Dragon Tours'

The dragons immediately took off, aiming for the opening from the market and they came so close to the upper part of the entrance that Angus had to duck as they flew through it. It was now getting dark as the sun was setting and on the left both protectors could see St Paul's in the distance; lit up against the skyline. The dragons pushed higher into the sky not bothering with dragon time and thus allowing the young humans to get a good look around. Looking behind them Angus could see the glass roof of Smithfield Market and beyond that three tall buildings standing in a line.

"That's the Barbican!" shouted Georgina pointing to the mass of concrete below the towers.

Angus nodded and wondered how she knew these things, but then again he guessed she must have been to London so many times on school trips and such like. The dragons began to gather speed as they flew west across the large city. The bend of the river drew nearer and Angus began to recognise features below that he knew. Trafalgar Square came into view with Nelsons Column looking just like a spike from the air, and

the ever present pigeons were mere dots on the ground. Soon the iconic Big Ben and Westminster Abbey were visible again thanks to some carefully placed floodlights. Georgina pointed out the London Eye ferris wheel as it dominated the South Bank of the River Thames opposite the Houses of Parliament. The dragons flew straight down a long tree-lined avenue and Buckingham Palace rolled into view. The Royal Standard was flying and Angus knew this meant the Queen must be at home. He could not help think that the dragons provided the best way to sight see and this could be a major tourist attraction if ever they were to come out of hiding!

Passing over Hyde Park the young protectors alighted from the Smithfield dragons at South Kensington. The finely crafted stonework of the Victorian edifice, which housed the Natural History Museum, was superbly lit and the stone carved animals and plants, which covered the building, were bathed in an eerie orange glow. Angus could not help but wonder at the effort that must have gone into the construction. He was reminded of his medieval adventure where he had seen first hand how these buildings were made and he had nothing but admiration for the skills of the stone masons of old.

"Thanks for the lift Hedley, you saved us loads of time" said Georgina smiling.

a long time.

"Yeah..." continued Angus rubbing his shoulder, "thanks!"

"The society has never found any dragons in the City before and it's fortunate that we've met you..." said Georgina buttering up the dragons some more, "you probably don't know this but the Great Hibernation has finally come to an end."

"Oh we all know about that dearie, we all saw old Barfoot in his message" threw in Latimer, matter-of-factly.

This surprised even Angus as most of the dragons had no recollection of the old Ward when he attempted to awaken them from their centuries' long slumber. Then Angus realised these dragons had not really been hibernating and therefore would not be suffering from the same kind of memory issues that the hibernating dragons had.

"I remember when he showed me to the Cor Stan and let me get my first piece of Dragonore... How is old Barfoot anyway?" asked Hedley.

The question brought back memories of the day Barfoot died in front of Angus. The old dragon had passed on the mantle of Ward to Godroi after the Trials and it was still a painful memory for the lad. He saw that Georgina was struggling not to cry and decided he had better answer.

in mock anger.

"Come on let's find my father before he starts to worry" she said as she pulled the arm of his jacket.

They saw the portly figure of the Vicar waiting on the steps of the Natural History Museum.

"Sorry we're a bit late Daddy" said Georgina as they approached him.

He did not seem at all surprised to have seen them disembark from the dragons' backs.

"I see you found some friendlier dragons… but the story will have to wait as we haven't got long… quickly, follow me" said the Vicar as he ushered them inside the revolving door of the Museum.

The trio stood in front of a large map of the galleries and Hugh suggested they choose what they wanted to see as they did not have much time before closing. Georgina wanted to see the enormous blue whale and so they made their way past the famous dinosaur skeleton in the Central Hall, and through the rooms containing reptiles and amphibians which none of them were particularly interested in. Hugh Penfold bobbed and weaved his way through the milling throngs of Christmas holiday visitors as Georgina and Angus explained how they had come to be on the backs of Hedley and Latimer.

"It sounds as if they acted just like those two fellows in that movie about the Highwaymen!" the Vicar chuckled, "What was it called again… Plankett and Mcleen?"

"Something like that Daddy… but the point is these dragons have been in London for hundreds of years and have had no contact from the SSDP in all that time!" she said rather too loudly.

A woman near to them looked at Georgina strangely and Angus caught her eye and smiled sweetly at her until she stopped being nosey and walked on.

Having viewed the large blue whale they decided to miss out the Earth hall and stuffed birds and insects due to the constraints of time but also because Angus was not particularly interested in those. What he really wanted to see was the famous moving Tyrannosaurus Rex model. As they crossed one of the upper landings Angus stopped to admire the vastness of the main entrance hallway with its high domed ceiling and intricate stonework.

"We haven't time to dawdle young man!" admonished the Vicar, who was already marching off in the direction of the Blue Zone, which housed the Museum's infamous dinosaurs.

The tannoy announced that the museum

would close in twenty minutes and this prompted the Vicar to speed up more; marching them into the dinosaur section and climbing the stairs to the raised walkways. He marched them passed a Diplodocus, an Allosaurus, an Iguanodon and a peaceful plant eater called a Tuojiangosaurus. These name labels passed in a blur and Angus would have liked to spend more time reading the information but the Vicar appeared to be on a mission! Georgina was now struggling to keep up thanks to her new boots and by now very sore feet. Suddenly they heard the famous working model of the mighty Tyrannosaurus Rex roaring around the next corner. Angus was amused to see little children putting their hands over their ears in fright upon hearing the roars of the dinosaur model despite their mother's soothing reassurances that it was not real. He also caught a glimpse of an information panel as he hurried past in the wake of the vicar, saying that said a Tyrannosaurus Rex weighed as much as twenty ten-year-old children! Georgina was clearly in pain and Angus insisted they stop to watch the T-Rex as it began to move its large head from side to side whilst it sniffed the air for fresh meat. The jaw line and sharp toothed mouth reminded Angus of a dragons and he wondered if they were somehow related to dinosaurs of old. These thoughts were purged as the T-Rex suddenly raised his large head and gave a blood curdling roar. This started all the young children squealing in a mixture of fear and awe as the computerised monster began its noisy show for the visitors.

"You have to admit it's pretty cool" said Angus turning to Georgina as she sat on a bench rubbing her feet.

"Yes... yes it's very nice, but there is something I want to show you both!" added the Vicar excitedly.

"Why don't you come up to the railing and have a closer look?" asked Angus ignoring her father for a second.

"No it's okay... let's go" she replied as she pushed her foot back into the offending boot with a grimace.

Soon they passed many more exhibits, all the time Georgina struggled to keep up with the portly vicar until, at last, he came to a triumphant halt in front of a pair of model nests. Angus had spotted other mechanical dinosaurs and was keen to go back, but in front of him now were the eggs of the Maiasaurus and Orodromeus dinosaur species.

"Look... down there!" the vicar jabbed his podgy finger towards one of the nests containing three eggs.

One of the eggs had already hatched with a replica baby dinosaur peeking out.

"Cool... Do they move?" asked Angus as he peered over the railing intently.

"Afraid not... but they are really interesting and very familiar, wouldn't you say?" he replied.

Angus nodded his agreement on that fact and began to read the label which suggested these particular species stayed either family groups and that sometimes un-hatched eggs were knocked over or trampled on by the newly hatched young in their hurry to leave the nest. Angus stared at the un-hatched eggs.

"They really do look like dragon eggs, don't they?" he said.

"I suppose so... they're not as veined though and a little bit smaller" replied Georgina joining in.

The trio discussed the egg similarities and started to debate whether dragons and dinosaurs were actually related.

"You know we're no nearer to finding the missing eggs and they are due to hatch very soon" said Angus suddenly.

'That assuming they are indeed safe somewhere!' he thought.

A polite but authoritative voice boomed over the tannoy, disrupting the discussion, telling them that the museum was now closing and instructing everybody to leave the building.

The trio reluctantly exited the museum and walked down the long pedestrian tunnel to the Underground station at South Kensington.

"Just before we leave London, Reverend Penfold, we need

to make one more visit… if we have enough time that is!" said Angus tentatively.

"Where could you possibly want to be going this late in the day?"

"I think Angus wants to try and talk to one of the other dragons before we go Daddy" suggested Georgina.

"Well the train leaves Blackfriars at 18:25, so make sure you are on the platform in time… I'll go on ahead and wait for you at the station…I could do with a cuppa and a bun" said the Vicar, ever mindful of his stomach.

Angus and Georgina hopped on the District and Circle line back towards the City because Angus wanted to visit Temple Bar again in the hope that he could speak to the dragon hiding there. Angus figured that if they could persuade enough of the others they could eventually win over the leader of the City Guardians. Around half an hour later both protectors stood across the street from the Temple Bar dragon and once again Angus detected a glimmer as they approached. This time there was no doubt that the inhabitant of the statue was at home as an angry black dragon wasted no time in morphing

out of the statue and confronting the pair on the dark and now deserted pavement.

"I told you two already, LEAVE US ALONE!"

Chapter 16

'Snap Dragon'

Confronted with the irate dragon, his demeanor threatening violence, Georgina stepped slightly behind Angus and held his arm. Angus looked into the snarling face and apart from the green eyes he could have been looking at Felspar; that's when the thought hit him.

"We've never had anything to do with the SSDP and we don't want you poking your noses in dragon business… I told you we look after the humans in this city and we're in charge around here" growled the dragon nastily.

"Faris, please… We're sorry if the mention of Felspar upset you, but the City Guardians should be pleased that he is no longer a threat to your leadership…" pleaded Angus.

"What do you mean he's no threat to us?" snapped the dragon, "How can you say that?"

"Well… it's kind of hard to explain…" replied Angus, "Can't you just trust me?"

"And why should we trust *you*?" spat the dragon.

"Because Angus saw him die!" blurted out Georgina, still fearful of the dragon looming over them.

Faris stared intently at Georgina's face looking for any sign of a lie, but her face reflected only the truth as she knew it. The leader of the City Guardians turned to Angus.

"Is this true, did you see him die?" asked Faris seriously.

Angus paused for a moment and recalled the events of that fateful day. The memory was so fresh in his mind it could have happened yesterday.

"Yes I did!"

"I must know. How did he die?" asked Faris eagerly.

Angus began to recall the events leading up to the day Felspar met his demise.

"Yes that sounds like the Felspar I know" said the dragon solemnly when Angus paused for breath.

The lad came to the final battle and he described it as only he could; in full detail and truthfully.

"...and then I ran forward with the broken sword and somehow I pierced his armour and drove the blade into his chest..." recalled Angus, "I killed him!" he said quietly.

Georgina let go of the lads arm as she spun around him to look her friend in the eye.

"YOU... you killed Felspar?" shouted the dragon incredulously.

Georgina's eyes were as round as dinner plates at this revelation. She knew of course that Felspar was dead, but like everyone else in the SSDP she thought that the knight George had killed him. The black dragon moved closer to Angus and stood square in front of him.

"Yes, I did and he's your brother, isn't he?" asked Angus. Now it was the dragon's turn to look surprised and Georgina looked from Angus to Faris trying desperately to keep up with the conversation and the revelations.

"Very astute of you young man… and yes he is my younger brother" replied the dragon regaining his composure. "Did you see him die?"

"Felspar was wounded through the chest and he hit me so hard I was knocked out!"

"So you didn't see him die?"

"No he sloped off to die… Pyrra and I searched for him once I regained consciousness but all we found were his jewels in the bottom of the stream" finished Angus.

Georgina still looked as though she had seen a ghost and Angus realised that he would have some explaining to do. It was only Rathlin, Finian, Ward Godroi and presumably Mrs T who knew the truth about that day. Angus always assumed that

Georgina had guessed the implications of the sword he had been left as a gift from the knight George. But obviously she had not and he now knew he had some apologies to make on the way home.

"I'm sorry for killing your brother!" said Angus quietly.

"I'm sorry that you had to kill him, but he would have killed you and your friends!" replied the dragon sadly.

The black dragon seemed to ponder the whole conversation and he walked to his statue just as a gap in the traffic allowed him to do so. Faris stood looking up at the proud stance of the statue as the traffic flow resumed. This stopped the protectors from joining him. They were invisible along with the dragon as long as they were close to him, which was just as well as the traffic had constantly passed them throughout the whole conversation. Eventually, another gap appeared and the two young protectors darted across to stand beside the large black dragon. Without any encouragement from the dragon, the pair pondered how they should end the silence.

"I am going to tell you one of the City Guardians greatest

secrets!" said Faris suddenly turning his head towards them. Angus and Georgina moved back slightly to allow the dragon to maneuver his body and face them.

"Jump on my back and I will explain on the way" he added.

"Where are we going?" asked Georgina.

"Don't worry it's not far but it will help you understand… for now, you must trust me!" replied the dragon.

With that said Angus jumped up and held out his hand to Georgina. She paused only for a split second before she grabbed his arm and allowed him to pull her up.

Faris took off and quickly spun over the rooftops of the Justice Courts and into the sky in the direction of St Paul's.

"This knowledge must only be known to you and the leaders of this Secret Society of yours…" spoke the dragon over his shoulder.

Both protectors nodded their agreement.

"Good… now listen carefully… no doubt some of the other dragons told you how Felspar was always trying to take over the leadership!" said the dragon.

"They only mentioned than you had some issues with him" replied Angus.

They had already passed over the top of the cathedral and were heading towards London

Bridge.

"Yes I certainly did and one day, several centuries ago, the pair of us fought on the north side of the river Thames… just on the edge of the City as it was back then" continued the dragon as he adjusted his wings to swing in towards the Monument they had visited earlier in the day. "We fought long and hard until eventually I subdued him. In the end I was forced to take his heart stone!"

"Godroi took his heart stone from him after the trials!" interjected Angus.

"Yes and I'm sure he deserved it and like the Ward, my intention was to render him powerless… otherwise he would just persist in challenging me and the whole hierarchy of the City dragons would have been threatened" continued the dragon as they swept around the Monument and landed at the base.

Georgina appeared to be very excited as they both jumped to the ground. She walked over to the large plaque they had read before and began to look for a certain part using her finger as a guide.

"Once I had won the battle fair and square, I went to snatch his heart stone to disarm him…" continued the dragon, "but he feigned acquiescence!"

"That's a tactic he's used very often, but he won't be using anymore!" said Angus soberly.

"Indeed. He caught me off guard!" said Faris, a look of self-admonishment on his face. "His flames engulfed me and I was forced to back away, but he cared not where he sprayed his flame and the thatched roof of a wooden bakery shop behind me caught fire!"

"I KNEW IT!" shouted Georgina, unable to keep quiet any longer. "I had an inkling a dragon had possibly started the fire, and what's more Sir Christopher Wren knew it too, it's on the base of The Monument!" she shrieked excitedly.

"You were correct in your suspicions young lady and Sir Christopher Wren was a very good friend to us by providing many places for us to hide" confirmed Faris.

"Why didn't you tell me your theory?" asked Angus slightly hurt, but then again he had kept the secret of Felspar from her so he could hardly complain.

Georgina did not have time to answer, but fixed him with an infuriated look and added this to her list of conversations to have with him later, as Faris continued with his story.

"As you have read, before we knew it the fire grew and spread until most of the City was destroyed!" said Faris sadly. "We tried to save as many as we could from the flames. We had been watching over London for many years protecting the inhabitants from as much harm as we could."

The large black dragon looked heartbroken and Angus realised that although they looked alike, the compassion Faris had for humans made him so different from his brother.

"What happened to Felspar?" asked Georgina.

"The coward slunk off not to be seen in the City again. A poor bakery boy was blamed for starting The Great Fire of London, but in truth it was Felspar" replied Faris, his eyes burning fiercely.

"And he never returned?" asked Georgina again.

"Never... and now my dear brother never will, thanks to this brave young man!" replied Faris, his eyes fixed on Angus. "We have kept watch for many years, always watching the skies for a black shadow. Just in case he ever returned to cause more pain and misery. But now we won't have to worry on that score."

The dragon then did something Angus had never seen him do before. He smiled!

Chapter 17

'Friendship Forged and Forgiven'

Georgina studied her best friend closely. She had seen Angus do many brave things, but this latest revelation of him having killed one of the fiercest dragons she had ever met was a real shock.

"We need you're help!" said Angus in an attempt to change the subject.

"The City Guardians are at your disposal" replied Faris with a slight bow of his head. "How can we be of assistance?"

Angus told the dragon leader about the missing eggs and all that had happened in the last week of searching.

"So you suspect they may be in London?" asked Faris with interest.

Angus thought of his earlier ideas about the scene he witnessed that morning. The strange woman and the two large men carrying the boxes into that building still niggled at him.

"Not really, but it won't do any harm to have some extra help… just in case" he replied.

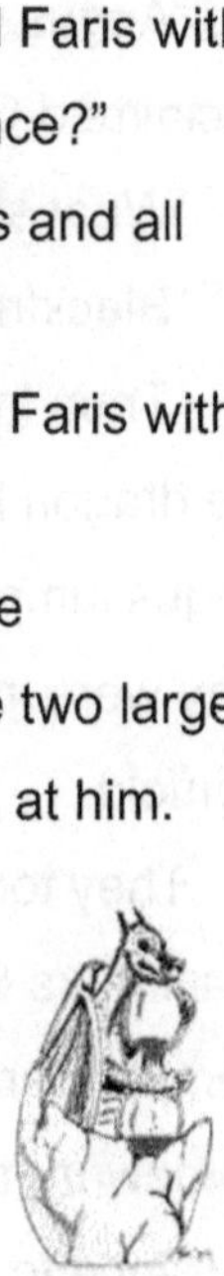

"Indeed it will not and I will call a meeting tomorrow and inform the City Guardians to be on the lookout for anything suspicious" said the large black dragon.

"So that's why you are all placed on the boundaries of the old city!" said Georgina.

"Yes and we have been here for so long, protecting the dwellers of this city from as many enemies as we can!"

"Just like protectors!" added Angus quietly.

"Indeed!" smiled the dragon.

A clock somewhere nearby chimed the hour and Georgina checked her watch.

"Angus we have to dash… the train leaves in 25 minutes!" exclaimed Georgina.

"What station are you leaving from?" asked Faris.

"Blackfriars!" replied Georgina anxiously.

"Then I will take you there… it is the least I can do" replied the dragon kneeling down to allow her to climb onto his back. Angus jumped up behind her and with a flick of dragon wings they were in the air and on their way to rendezvous with Hugh Penfold.

They took their leave of the leader and he flew from Blackfriars Station heading back to his hiding place inside the Temple Bar Dragon. They were just about in time to catch the homeward train, and Georgina's father was waiting at the entrance to the platform pacing up and down.

"Ah there you are at last!" he called to them as they approached. "I was beginning to worry!"

"Sorry Daddy but we had a slight detour" said Georgina giving him a hug.

"Well I hope it was worth the effort?" he asked.

"Totally!" replied Angus smiling.

"Yes, we've some interesting things to tell you on the journey home" added Georgina looking at Angus.

"Well then I cannot wait, but let's procure ourselves good seats before you start" said the Vicar leading the way to the platform.

On the train back to Marnham Georgina had given her father a run down of the day's main events and what had happened after they parted company outside the museum. This would not have taken so long had it not been for his constant interruptions of 'You don't say' and 'Well I never'. Angus was deep in thought, 'What a day it had been! So many dragons discovered in the City; So much to tell Rathlin and Pyrra'. His mind reeled with it all as the tidying part of his brain tried to put it in order.

"Well now all this excitement has made me peckish… anyone for a slice of cake? Crisps, juice… It's no trouble!" asked the Vicar as he

stood up.

The train was busy with weary commuters returning home late from the City, but they were lucky to get a seat together and Georgina took her chance to have a private conversation with her best friend.

"So you killed Felspar?" she asked, accusingly.

Angus looked into her face and could see she was hurt by the secrecy of the whole thing.

"I wanted to tell you... but Rathlin made me promise..."

Even as he said the words he knew they sounded lame. When had he ever been scared to bend the rules!

"Sorry..." he whispered.

Georgina looked at the friend who had saved her life on at least a couple of occasions and who would put himself in danger to avoid any friend from being hurt. She did not know anyone else as selfless or as modest as he was and she doubted she ever would.

"It's okay Angus... I forgive you..." she replied and then seeing his face light up, "but I was a little miffed at first!" she ended smiling at him.

The lad was relieved that he was off the hook, but she forced him to recount the whole episode in as much detail as he could remember. Georgina sat fascinated by the whole story, as

Angus left no detail untold. In fact he had never explained the fight to anyone like this before and it felt good to get it off of his chest.

"You must have used dragon time to have managed to build up enough speed in that short a distance…" interjected Georgina intuitively, "How did you manage to do that?" she asked.

Angus thought about this. In fact he had thought about it every day since and for the life of him he could not figure out how he had done it. What he did know was he would not stop until he had figured it out. Somehow he had been able to tap into the power of the dragons and the power of the Cor Stan.

"I wish I knew!" he replied.

"Well when you do find out, make sure you tell me this time" she added, grinning at him.

With no sign of the Vicar yet they chatted on about what had happened that day and what it all meant to the SSDP. Angus could not wait to tell Rathlin and Mrs T about this latest group of dragons, and hoped to return soon with leader of the SSDP to help convince the City Guardians of the Society's best intentions.

"What did you make of the fight between Faris and Felspar?" asked Georgina.

"Typical Felspar… Always after the power that others have…" replied Angus, "but I'll tell you one thing, it must have been some battle!"

"All those poor people died because of Felspar's lust for power… I'm glad he's not around to cause any more trouble!" said the girl, frowning.

"Yeah me too…" added Angus thoughtfully, "The world is certainly better off without him and thankfully his brother seems to think so too!"

Angus looked up the aisle and saw the vicar coming towards them. The he remembered something that Faris had said.

"So do you think that Sir Christopher Wren was a protector?"

"Wren, a protector… Now that's an interesting idea!" replied Georgina.

"Well he did look after the dragons and Faris said that Wren knew about their existence, so it wouldn't surprise me if he was in the SSDP" explained Angus.

"You could be right…" she replied excitedly, then turning to her father as he arrived. "Daddy we have something really interesting to tell you…"

Chapter 18

'Unwilling Promise'

While they discussed the possibility of Sir Christopher Wren being a protector the train sped on through the darkness, illuminated by the lights of a town or village as it swept on into the countryside. In no time at all, the train pulled into Marnham station already half empty as many passengers had already alighted. They trio made for the exit and Angus jumped down excitedly onto the concrete platform scanning the surroundings for Pyrra. As the train pulled away he spotted her on the roof of the signal box, unseen of course by anyone on the train or the platform. The dragon had not spotted him yet and he took a moment to say goodbye to Georgina and to thank her father. He watched them go out through the ticket office to the station car park and collect the vicar's ancient Mini Mayfair, which was extremely difficult for the portly Vicar to get into. Angus smiled as he watched Hugh twist and shuffle his body into the driver's seat until he was firmly wedged behind the small steering wheel. Even from the platform he could hear the Vicar harrumphing as the engine turned over a few times. The old car did not take well to being left in a cold exposed car park all day.

"Had a good outing then?" said a voice behind him and giving him a start.

"Oh... er... Yeah, we did!" replied Angus turning to see Pyrra standing right behind him in the middle of the platform. "I was just coming to get you..."

"That's fine... I was getting bored on top of that roof... There are only so many trains you can watch you know!" replied Pyrra smiling.

"Any news on Rhys' eggs?" he asked.

"None I'm afraid" replied the green dragon shaking her head. "Wymarc and I spent the whole day together searching and speaking to as many dragons as we could!"

Angus did not reply, as he felt down hearted at the lack of news on the eggs whereabouts. In fact they had not even heard so much as a whisper about them and that was more frightening than anything else. He was beginning to think they would never see nor hear of the eggs ever again.

Angus nestled on Pyrra's back and having been asked what he did in London he was soon in full flow, recounting the day's adventures. Before long, Pyrra had heard everything from the empty boundary statues, to meeting the City Guardians at Smithfield. Additionally Angus gave an account of what they saw at the museum, including the dinosaur eggs, and the final conversation with Faris. He was tired from the long day but the excitement of recounting all that had happened was keeping him awake. The only thing he did not tell her was the bit when he had thought he had seen Meredith and the eggs.

"Could you ever get used to chilled meat?" he asked once he had finished the story of Faris and Felspar's battle.

"I expect it's an acquired taste born of necessity…" replied the bemused dragon, "but I doubt I could do it for long!" The dragon, more so than any other being, understood Angus because of the connective bond they had formed over the last year and so she knew he had not told her everything that had happened that day. She also knew he probably had good reason for not telling her just yet, and that he would do so when he was ready.

The next morning, whilst Angus sat contemplating a bowl of cereal, his father, sat across the breakfast table buttering toast, actually acknowledged his son's presence in the room.

"What's on your mind son?"

"Uh…" said Angus completely taken by surprise, "Oh nothing" he replied gaining his composure after such an unusual event.

Angus' mother was behind him at the sink and she

turned and made encouraging gestures at her husband to continue the conversation.

"Are… you sure son?" asked Donald reluctantly persistent, "Perhaps I can help?"

Angus paused for a second, thrown by this unexpected but pleasant experience of being able to have a conversation with his normally quiet father; then he thought better of it.

"I want to find out if someone I know works in London" replied Angus looking serious.

"Is this a friend of yours?" asked his dad smiling at Angus' mother who looked very smug indeed.

"Sort of" replied Angus slowly.

"What do you know anything about this friend?" asked Donald warming to the task.

"I know she works in a building near St Paul's" said the lad still trying to figure out how his dad could possibly help.

"Okay… St Paul's eh… any idea what the building is called?"

"Halcyon House I think" replied Angus.

Donald Munro was so pleased that his son was communicating with him that he did not think to ask the lad why on earth he wanted such information. Instead he pushed his open laptop across the breakfast table and directed Angus to a website specialising in company listings. His father joined him on the other side of the table and he clicked on a site in his 'favourites'. It was a business directory and Donald wasted no time in showing Angus where to input the search criteria. Angus typed in the name of the building and clicked 'search' with the pointer. After a few seconds of processing time, a list of companies appeared on the screen.

"There you go son" said Donald triumphantly.

"Cool… thanks dad!" replied Angus as he scanned the list. It was a large building and as it turned out there were two other buildings called Halcyon House. This made the list rather long and Angus began to scan the eleven pages containing all the companies that were listed.

Three pages into the list Angus had still not found what he was looking for. In fact he was not sure he would find it, but at least it would satisfy his insatiable appetite to get to the bottom of a problem. He had clicked on a couple of possibilities and unfortunately not seen anything on the home pages that would make him go further.

"Any luck son?" asked his dad coming back to the table from the sink.

"Not yet dad" replied the lad dejectedly as he clicked for page four.

"Keep looking..." encouraged his dad, "I'm sure this site will have what you're looking for!"
Angus scanned the next lot on the page and scrolled down to the part of the list that was hidden. His eyes locked on an oil and gas drilling company and he remembered a conversation he had heard sometime ago. Meredith had been telling someone she ran a drilling company she had inherited from her father. He looked at the name of the company, the mouse pointer hovering over it as he read the short sentence that described the name and type of business they did. 'QJD Limited specialised in worldwide drilling operations for all major oil and gas companies.' It did not seem very helpful but he clicked the left mouse button anyway. The home page had an array of pictures that flashed up on the screen at regular intervals as the metallic company logo revolved slowly in the middle. The large interlinked QJD drew his attention and he clicked the mouse again in the middle of the logo. The screen flashed up with the company profile and introduction, which Angus quickly scanned past as his eyes were drawn to the section below.

'CEO's WELCOME AND COMMITMENT'

At the beginning of that paragraph was a picture of the owner, director and CEO; one Meredith Quinton-Jones.

"YES!" said Angus as he punched the air.

"Did you find it?" asked Angus' father.

"Yeah, thanks Dad!" he called as he clicked on the companies contact details. Her drilling company had its headquarters in London and satellite offices in Houston, Singapore, and Dubai. They occupied the top two floors of Halcyon House and had been there for 25 years. Angus made some mental notes, closed the page and snapped the laptop shut. As he jumped up from the table he gave his dad a rough hug, the gesture catching Donald Munro by surprise, but leaving him pleased to have made a breakthrough with his usually uncommunicative thirteen year old son.

Angus knew exactly what he wanted to do next and he needed to see Pyrra as quickly as possible. He was half way up the stairs when the phone rang.

"Angus, it's for you dear!" called his mother.
He leapt down again to answer.

"Hi Angus, I just wanted to know how you are feeling after yesterday?" asked Georgina.

"Yeah, fine... You're up early!"

"Oh I've got an early choir practice in a minute... I just thought maybe you were still thinking about those boxes" she continued.

The hair on the back of his neck prickled and he wondered if she was reading his mind or had some sort of sixth sense, in common with his dragon friend.

"What makes you think I would still be upset about that?" he asked trying to sound innocent.

"Well you were quite adamant at lunch and I understand you well enough to know you don't give up that easily" she replied truthfully.

"I did have a look at a business directory to see what companies used that building" he replied cautiously.

"I knew you wouldn't give up that easily… you are so stubborn. Well, what did you find out?" she asked.

"Meredith's company headquarters is in that building and I was just on my way to tell Pyrra" replied the lad getting excited.

"Look Angus you just can't go accusing Meredith of stealing the eggs without proof… Please stop and think about this or you'll get yourself in trouble!" said Georgina trying to calm him down a little.

They both knew that he was motivated by his gut feelings and because he was so desperate to help Rhys trace her eggs his judgment might well be clouded. Both were mindful of the fact that the eggs would soon be hatching and it would be disastrous if this historic event were to happen outside of the jurisdiction of the Secret Society of Dragon Protectors.

"Angus, promise me you won't do anything without talking to me!" she pleaded.

Reluctantly the lad agreed not to do anything without letting her know what the planned course of action was and promising that she would be included in anything he and Pyrra did. As soon as the conversation ended he ran back upstairs to get ready for a chilly bike ride to Piggleston; he could not wait to tell Pyrra about his discovery!

Chapter 19

'A Plan is Hatched'

The Piggleston sign came into view as Angus freewheeled around a bend and into the last stretch of road that led to the village. He had managed to cycle there in record time and immediately let Pyrra know he needed to talk to her. She obviously sensed his excited urgency, as by the time he had sped to the usual meeting place in the trees, she was already waiting for him.

"You look tired young man" she commented.

"I'm... fine... just a... little out... of breath!" he panted in reply.

The young lad soon regained control and began to explain about what he thought he had seen the day before.

"Why didn't you tell me this yesterday?" asked Pyrra.

"To be honest I was convinced by the others that I had been mistaken and I didn't want you to think I was trying see things that weren't there" replied Angus truthfully.

"And when have I ever doubted you?" asked the dragon kindly. "So can I assume you have a good reason for telling me now?"

Angus looked into the large green eyes of his best friend and realised he could tell her anything in truth and she would believe him. He would never tell her a lie and she would probably know if he did anyway, but sometimes he did not tell her everything. This was not one of those times and he began to tell Pyrra what he found out on the Internet.

"So you think you saw Meredith and her bodyguards with the eggs and now you want to go and check it out… correct?" asked the green dragon with a wry smile.
Angus just smiled and nodded his head enthusiastically; he really did love Pyrra.

"Then what are we waiting for… let's go!" replied the dragon bending to allow him to jump onto her back.

"Wait there's something else…" said the lad hurriedly explaining about his promise to Georgina.

"She knows you too well Angus…" laughed Pyrra, "I suppose we had better go to Marnham and persuade her to come to London with us!"

"I just want to find the eggs before the Fire Whelps hatch!" said the young protector.

"Then let's see if we can discover what Meredith's up to and perhaps these City Guardians can help us!" replied the green dragon.

With that said and a flap of her wings they were off on the familiar journey to Marnham.

Arriving at the Vicarage, they found no-one at home and headed to St George's church where they discovered Georgina deeply engrossed in choir practice for a winter wedding. As they approached the church they could hear the sweet sounds of young voices blending in harmony as they sang.

"That's funny… Argent's not here" said Pyrra immediately noticing the absence of her music-loving friend.

Wymarc silently morphed out of the stained glass window that Godroi used to inhabit and greeted the pair as they walked across the grass.

"Good morning Pyrra, I really did not expect to see you so soon but it's a wonderful surprise none the less" said the blue dragon.

"Good morning Wymarc we have SSDP business to take care of and we need your help…" replied the dragon, "where's Argent?"

"He's really distraught about the missing eggs. Even listening to music has not been able to temper the guilt he feels and every day since he has been out searching" replied the blue dragon sadly.

"I will need to have a chat with him when he returns… did

he say when he would be back?"

"No, but he always returns very late in the night and is off again in the early morning... he looks terrible but nothing I say seems to make any difference" replied Wymarc.

Pyrra looked very unhappy to hear that one of her oldest friends was in such a bad state and it pained her more that she had not been aware of it. She had been neglectful of him since the search began, as well as her new friendship with Wymarc.

"So what is this SSDP business that I can help you with?" asked Wymarc breaking her train of thought.

The green dragon began to explain the situation and what they planned to do about it.

"Of course I would be extremely happy to help and I am dying to meet these City Guardians myself after what Georgina told me about them" replied the male dragon enthusiastically. It was not long before the two dragons began to talk about other subjects and the conversation became something from which Angus felt excluded. Georgina and the rest of the choir had begun to exit the church and she waved to him when he called her name. As Angus went to meet her he turned to Pyrra and looking at the body language of the two dragons the thought suddenly occurred to him that recruiting Georgina

for this mission was not Pyrra's only motive for coming to Marnham.

The young female dragon protector waved goodbye to her friends and then turned to greet Angus as he approached.

"Hi Angus..." she said, "Why didn't you tell me on the phone earlier that you were coming?"

"I didn't know I was" he replied sheepishly.

"Okay, so why *are* you here?" she asked suspiciously.

"I told Pyrra about Meredith and she wanted to go and check it out for herself" he replied feeling like he was in trouble with one of his teachers. "I also told her that you made me promise to tell you if we were going to do anything and she suggested we take you and Wymarc along" he continued, smiling cheekily.

Georgina leaned to one side of Angus to give herself a better view of the two dragons behind him.

"Yes I noticed she and Wymarc were getting very friendly!"

"Oh c'mon Georgina, it'll be fun... and Wymarc's happy to go!" added Angus in an effort to appeal to her adventurous side.

She looked at him sternly for a few seconds making him think she was unhappy about the proposal; then she smiled broadly and nodded her approval.

It did not take long for Georgina to get ready, but she had to sneak past her father, as she was sure he would not approve of her disappearing up to the City without him. The two dragons silently took to the skies and flew the protectors southeast towards London. With the help of dragon time the journey was a bit quicker than by train and the River Thames gradually grew in size as it rolled out before them like an intricate carpet. Now the city's famous landmarks became more apparent, readily seen from the air. Two of the most prominent were Canary Wharf's tall tower, and the gigantic ferris wheel that was The London Eye. This was already busy with tourists queuing to ride the world-renowned landmark. Angus directed Pyrra towards the Temple Bar area and the street where they had met Faris. Moving out of dragon time the dragons floated down lightly by using their wings to slowly descend into the middle of the busy road.

The protectors and dragons were very careful not to get in the way of any traffic as it passed either side of the island that housed the statue in the centre of the street.

Angus jumped down from Pyrra's back and walked up to the base of the black statue.

"He's not here!" he said.

"Perhaps he's at Smithfield Market?"

suggested Georgina.

"And perhaps he is standing behind you!" replied a gruff voice.

Chapter 20

'Attentive Congregation'

Dragons and protectors spun round in the direction of the voice to find the black dragon standing proudly before them.

"Good morning Angus..." said Faris, "I'm surprised to see you back so soon, and with guests... Please allow me to introduce myself; I am Faris, leader of the City Guardians!" finished the black dragon with a bow.

"Faris this is Wymarc and this is Pyrra" replied Angus, remembering that dragons enjoyed the formality and importance of introductions.

"You cannot imagine how pleased I am to meet two more dragons after all this time!" said Faris who looked at Pyrra with interest.

"And we are equally pleased to meet you!" said Wymarc standing tall as if on his guard.

"Indeed, as you will find the rest of the Guardians will be most interested in meeting both of you; especially you Pyrra!" said Faris returning his gaze to appraise her.

Angus remembered that the London dragons were all male and had not seen a female for hundreds of years. Pyrra would no doubt love the attention but he hoped it would not cause any problems with the blue dragon who seemed to be very possessive of her all of a sudden.

"I think it would be better to reconvene at Smithfield and I will alert the rest of the City Guardians" suggested Faris.

"How long will it take to get them together?" asked Georgina.

"Not long at all" replied the black dragon smiling.

That said, he tilted his head back and stretched his neck as high as he could. At first it did not appear that the dragon would do anything else, but then a low pitched sound began to emanate from the dragon's mouth. The noise grew in intensity until it was quite audible above the mechanical hum of the buses and cars. The resonance of the sound became stronger and louder until the point where Angus could see people walking on the pavements look up and around them. Luckily the dragons were invisible and also the protectors, due to their proximity to the dragons but Angus could not help wonder if Faris' actions were wise. It was plain to all that they had just heard a long and drawn out roar but how it was made was anyone's guess. Faris stopped and lowered his head with his eyes closed.

"Shall we go then?" he asked suddenly opening his bright green eyes.

"What was that you just did?" asked Georgina.

"Why I called them to the meeting of course!" replied Faris looking puzzled. "Is that not something you do?" he asked Pyrra.

"No… In fact I've never seen that before…" she replied, "How did you do it?"

"I slowed the muscles in my throat to allow the sound to be drawn out" he replied.

"I didn't know we could use dragon time in that way" replied Pyrra.

"Dragon time?" asked Faris puzzled.

"Yes… it's the name Angus gave our ability to speed up or slow down time" she answered.

"That's very good…" said Faris thoughtfully, "I like that!" he added turning to Angus who went red with embarrassment.

"Why is it necessary?" asked Wymarc.

"Well, it keeps the roar from being too recognisable and the resonance allows the others to distinguish the call from other background noise" replied the black dragon, "This is a very busy city!"

"It was well cool" said Angus recovering his composure slightly, "Will it work?"

"Thank you and I have no doubt they will already be on their way…" replied Faris smiling at the young lad, "Shall we go?"

Both protectors mounted up and Faris led the visitors up into the sky above Temple Bar in the direction of Smithfield.

They swept into the large covered area where Angus and Georgina had discovered the City Guardians previously discussing the presence of two humans with Dragonore, and found two dragons already waiting. Latimer and Hedley, Smithfield market's resident dragons, were having a discussion but stopped abruptly as Faris led the others to the meeting place. Angus could see that some of the meat traders were cleaning up the last of their activities oblivious to the presence of five dragons not even thirty feet away.

"Well now dearie, are you a sight for sore eyes and no mistake!" cried Latimer.

"Too right Lovey!" chimed in Hedley.

"Right you two that will be enough of that nonsense!" barked Faris.

The black dragon did not finish because up swept Lothair through the Grand Avenue and landed heavily beside Latimer and Hedley and greeted them before looking at Faris questioningly.

"Lothair you have obviously met Georgina and Angus before, but this is Wymarc and Pyrra!" said Faris in introduction to the red dragon.

All the dragons made the usual greetings after Faris introduced Latimer and Hedley, explaining that they lived in the market and that Lothair hid in The Monument near King William Street on London Bridge. As this was happening Dhruv silently joined the burgeoning collection of dragons and when he was introduced they found out he was the dragon they'd detected from the train at Blackfriars Bridge. He was a light grey green colour and very timid. In fact he had said nothing at all during the introductions and Angus wondered if he would speak at all. Next was Fulbert, the gold dragon from St Mary le Bow who was a lot friendlier this time, closely followed by Kennard from London Bridge, Lyell from Guildhall and Wulfric from Holborn Viaduct. By the time proper introductions had been made,

Pyrra's presence was causing quite a stir amongst the all male dragon gang and the new allies were giving her a lot of attention.

"As you can see, the young protectors were telling the truth, and they have indeed become the friends of dragons like us" said Faris after he called the City Guardians to order, "They have asked for our help in a matter of grave importance and I would like to ask Angus to speak."

The young lad had not expected this invitation and at first was not sure where he should start but he began with how the Society worked and explained a bit more fully about The Secret Society of Dragon Protectors; the missing dragon eggs and his suspicions about Meredith Quinton Jones.

"So we need all of you to keep an eye on Halcyon House as Meredith might have something to do with the disappearance" he finished.

"How did you become a dragon protector then?" asked Wulfric shiftily as he found it hard to trust the newcomers.

Angus informed the dragons how he had awakened Pyrra in the children's ride outside the sweet shop and about the resurgence of the Society. After further prompting he explained about the Trials of the Cor Stan. During all of this Georgina found the whole situation very amusing indeed as once again she was subjected to Hedley stroking her hair with his fore claw. Angus described the Trials one by one and Felspar's foul play was met with jeers.

"It's just like him to do something like that" said Kennard gruffly.

Faris looked knowingly at Angus as he was the only City Guardian that knew the truth about Felspar. The dragons confessed they had received the message to awaken from Ward Barfoot but they had not really been in hibernation and not bothered to answer the call. Angus went on to explain about Barfoot and his successor Ward Godroi living deep in the caves at Krubera, and also about the Tek brothers and their leadership of the Society. There were collective mutterings about the passing of Barfoot and approval of Godroi as the new Ward. The congregated dragons made many appreciative nods in the direction of Pyrra in recognition of her part in the defeat of Felspar. Angus assured them he would get Rathlin to come and introduce himself as the Head of the SSDP next time they visited.

"So will we help them?" asked Faris once Angus had finished.

A few of the dragons shifted uneasily or looked sideways at each other.

"Of course we'll help dearie!" shouted Latimer.

"We could do with a bit of excitement round here lovey..." added Hedley, "nothing out of the ordinary ever happens in this dull city!"

Faris shook his head in exasperation, as the other dragons roared their approval.

Chapter 21

'Watcher's Watched'

A few hours later Angus stood with Pyrra on the eastern end of St Paul's roof watching the curved building opposite that was Halcyon House. The majority of the dragons had left the meeting and Faris had allowed Latimer and Hedley to accompany the visitors to take the first watch.

"Do you think she's in there now?" asked Georgina getting restless.

"I don't know but I guess we will just need to keep watch to make sure" replied Angus.

Georgina peered over the stonework of the roof they were sat on and stared at the windows of the building.

"Which floors did you say she was on again?"

"The top two" replied Angus dourly.

"This is silly..." said Georgina as she shook her head, "we don't even know if she has the eggs or not and why keep them here when she could move them to her country house?"

Angus knew she was right but he was too stubborn to admit it and thought desperately for some reason to justify his actions.

"She knew we would come to check on her there" he replied unconvincingly, "and my guess is she thinks we don't know about this place!"

Even Angus was struggling to believe his own reasons for being on this freezing cold roof right now and as he saw Pyrra flying back with Wymarc he hoped she would have some positive news.

"Did you see anything?" he asked eagerly.

"Nothing at all... and we flew around the back several times before we gave up" replied Pyrra shaking her head.

Angus slumped down on the roof with his back to the small stonework wall that crowned the top of the building. Georgina walked over and sat beside him.

"Don't worry Angus we'll find the eggs" she said trying to reassure him.

Suddenly Hedley and Latimer landed on the roof beside them.

"Watcha!" shouted Hedley as he landed.

"Guess what we saw dearie!" cried Latimer as he landed behind them.

"What, the eggs?" asked Angus hopefully.

"No lovey, we saw a lovely purple coat...it would really suit you!"

"Wouldn't it just dearie!" added Latimer.

Angus slumped down again dejected and the two dragons looked at each other.

"We did see two men on the roof smoking and then they went back inside" replied Hedley.

"That doesn't sound like much help" said Wymarc.
The young protectors did not think so either.

"Let's go home Angus..." said Georgina, "It's lunchtime and I'm cold and the boys can watch the place for us... Won't you?"

"Of course we will lovey" replied Hedley.

"Sure dearie, you two get off home and leave everything to us" added Latimer.
Pyrra placed a claw reassuringly on Angus' shoulder and he looked up into large green eyes. Without a word he knew what she was telling him and he reluctantly stood and climbed onto her back. They waited for Georgina to say goodbye to Latimer and Hedley as she had grown extremely fond of this bizarre pair of dragons, and their comic antics.

The Cathedral fell away behind them as Angus watched it roll over the horizon. He turned to face forward; his mind reeled with thoughts about the eggs and Meredith. Assuming they had been kept warm they would hatch in less than a week and he could only imagine what might happen to them

after that. He knew Meredith had planned to take over the SSDP and use the dragons for some purpose of her own, but would a successful businesswoman really stoop to common theft? The dark blue dragon that had haunted his dreams during the hunt for Felspar had stayed absent these past few months, and he had been glad of the peace, but now he wished it would return to give him some clue or help as to the whereabouts of the eggs. Clearly that was not going to happen!

They flew onwards to the outskirts of London and Angus watched the M25 ebb and flow with traffic like a major artery to a heart. He saw two men arguing by the side of the road, gesticulating towards their cars, both of which had damage. A police car, blue lights flashing, picked its way carefully through the busy traffic in an attempt to find the blockage and remove it. All of this was a welcome distraction for the young protector and he maintained his focus on this scene until they were well past it. It became difficult to see what was happening now and he was about to return to a forward looking position when he noticed something in the thin clouds behind him. At first he thought it was his imagination but then he realised what he was seeing and spun around.

"Pyrra, slow down!" he shouted.

Both Pyrra and Wymarc immediately came out of dragon time

and turned to the young protector for an explanation but before he could say anything Latimer appeared out of dragon time between both of the dragons.

"Thanks heavens for that!" he said. "I thought you were never going to stop dearie!"

"What's the matter?" asked Pyrra clearly concerned.

"Well dearie you know us two, quiet and unassuming, wouldn't know we were there most of the time would you..." said Latimer as Georgina giggled behind her hand. "Anyway we saw someone up at one of those big windows on the top floor and we were looking up and then we realised this woman was watching us too! Well dearie that was a shock coz we're not used to humans having Dragonore, but she definitely clocked the two of us and no mistaking!"

"Did she have dark hair?" asked Angus urgently.

"Oh yes dearie, lovely it was. Long and black... but not as nice as yours dearie" he replied turning to Georgina who brushed the compliment aside.

"What happened then?" asked Angus desperately.

"Now dearie that was the strange thing... nothing happened... she just smiled and then closed her curtain."

Angus thought frantically about Meredith and how she would react to this discovery. On the one hand she may be innocent and assume that the SSDP were just keeping an eye on her, but on the other hand she may well be guilty and would no doubt move the eggs after being tipped off.

"We have to go back!" said Angus.

"And do what?" asked Georgina wondering what scheme he had thought up now.

"I'm not sure yet but I'll tell you when we get there… just trust me… please!" he replied looking at Pyrra for support. His companion and best friend just nodded trustingly and with a simple tilt of her wings turned back towards London.

Chapter 22

'Smoke and Mirrors'

They dropped lightly onto the roof of St Paul's where Hedley waited patiently for them.

"Watcha lovey... you found them then?" he said grinning.

"Of course I did dearie!" smiled Latimer.

Angus jumped from Pyrra's back and scanned the top floor of the building opposite.

"Which window was it?" he asked.

"Oh now let me see… that one" replied Latimer.

"No lovey… it was that one" corrected Hedley.

"Are you sure dearie?" said the slate coloured dragon looking thoughtful.

"Absolutely lovey… I haven't taken my eyes off that building for a second… well except when this gorgeous young lady came walking down the street with the most lovely blonde hair" replied Hedley, "'Cept not as nice as yours lovey!" he added to Georgina who gave him a shove.

Angus knew the dragons would prattle on like this for some time and he turned to Pyrra.

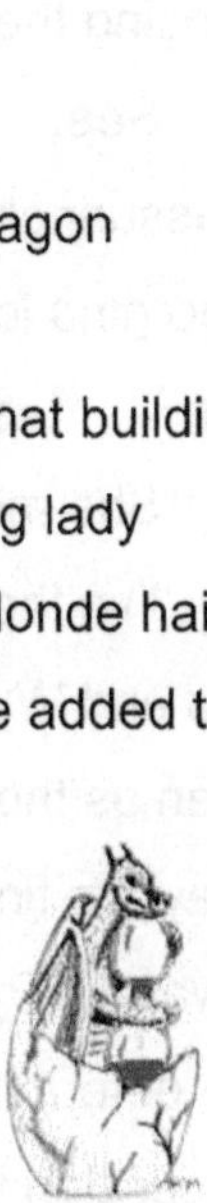

"Can you take me up to the roof and drop me on it?" he asked urgently.

"NO... Angus it's much too dangerous!" cried Georgina. "Let's go and get help from the SSDP first!" she suggested looking very concerned.

"There's no time" he replied. "If we don't act now we may never know if the eggs are there or not!"

"But even if they were, she might have already moved them" replied the girl logically.

"Has anyone left the building since Meredith saw you?" he asked turning to Hedley.

"No lovey... not a soul" replied the dragon suddenly sensing the seriousness of the situation.

"See... and I'm only going to take a look around" he replied reassuringly.

Georgina looked to Pyrra for support and the dragon took her cue.

"She might detect your Dragonore Angus" she ventured.

"I've thought of that... If Hedley and Latimer stay here and you and Wymarc stay on the roof then any detection will be seen as them. Since she already knows they are here I will be okay" he finished with a triumphant look on his face.

Inwardly, Pyrra had to commend his ingenuity and judging by the determined look on his face she realised any further discussion would be futile.

"Okay... but I will only take you if you promise not to try anything silly!" replied the green dragon.

"COOL!" shouted Angus excitedly. "C'mon then, let's go before she sees us!"

Georgina wanted to object but all she could do was stand with her mouth open as Angus jumped up onto Pyrra's back. She followed suit and climbed up onto Wymarc before reluctantly waving goodbye to the two Smithfield dragons.

They hovered above the flat roof and Angus surveyed it from Pyrra's back. There were three higher sections that housed the access doors or fire escapes. He looked for a way into the building, but none of the doors had any handles on the outside and he could see no other way in. Next to the fire escape buildings was a multitude of metallic silver air ducting that served as the ventilation system to the building. The exhaust fans spun quietly on top of the mirror-like sheet metal ducting and Angus considered this as a possible means of entry.

"Let's land on top of the fire escape roof so I can have a closer look" he said to Pyrra.

He jumped down onto the hard surface and leant over the edge to get a better look at the door below him. It had ducts on either side and it was clear that the door was only meant to be opened from the inside. He remembered Latimer and Hedley had said that two men had been smoking on the roof and sure enough he could see countless cigarette butts stamped into the tarred surface around the doorway. Georgina and Wymarc hovered nearby and Angus turned to indicate they should wait further away.

"Be careful" she warned in a whisper.

With a wave, Wymarc swept off to the other end of the building and landed behind another doorway.

Suddenly the door below flew open and banged against the wall. Angus quickly ducked back as two burly men walked through the doorway and stepped out onto the roof. Angus could hear them talking and from the smell they had obviously lit cigarettes. Pyrra wrinkled her nose in disgust and Angus put his sleeve over his nose, as he did not like cigarette smoke either. Waving Pyrra back he lay down on the small roof of the building and slowly edged forward to allow him to spy on the two men. Angus held his breath and listened to them discussing their boss in not very affectionate tones.

"Did you hear the way she spoke to me just then?" said the larger of the two.

"Yeah she's a real tyrant that one… been brought up used to everyone running after her" replied the other man.

"Told me I was an idiot an all... I mean what's that all about then?" added the big man before taking another puff of his cigarette.

"Spoiled if you ask me... Still the money's good though!" added the other man.

Angus was sure he recognised them from the incident in the street the other day and he quickly realised his only way into the building was through the doorway they had just come through. Somehow he had to get through it whilst the men were still on the roof. The drop to the lower level was too high for him to jump down and the only other way was onto the ducting, which would surely make a noise. He had a plan but he would need Pyrra's help so he carefully slid back to speak to her.

"Listen, this is what I need you to do..." he whispered as he began to explain exactly how he would get inside.

The dragon listened intently and began to wonder if he was mad but then, she knew him better than that.

Angus waited patiently for his opportunity to appear which would happen as soon as Pyrra was able to do as he had asked. He watched her take off, fly to the opposite side of the building before she quietly maneuvered around the roof keeping well out of sight of the two men. Just as expected, a

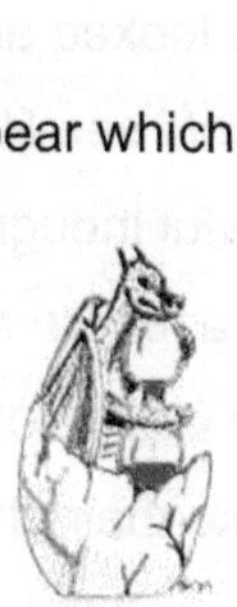

crashing noise came from the end that faced the doorway. Both men stopped mid discussion and stared at the fire escape at that end the noise came from.

"Did you hear that Jeff?" asked one of them.

"Well of course I did you idiot... who wouldn't?" snarled the other man.

"Maybe we should check it out like... you know seeing as we're security an' all" suggested the larger of the two.

The men stamped out their cigarettes and cautiously walked toward the other doorway. The plan had worked and Angus waited until they were about halfway to the spot where Pyrra now hid.

Seizing his moment he spun his body over the edge of the small roof and lowered himself to the ducting below. He was at full stretch hanging by his fingers when he realised that the drop was a foot or two more than he had thought. Desperately he looked at the men as they neared the other doorway. He could see Pyrra peeking from behind the building when an awful thought struck him. He hoped the men did not have any Dragonore as they would surely see her if they did. He realised he could not worry about that now and they would have to just take their chances as he was now committed to getting inside the building. He also knew he would make a loud noise when he dropped onto the sheet metal and it was only a matter of time before his fingers would lose grip. He had no choice but to let go and try to land as lightly as possible.

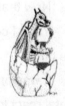

Chapter 23

'Dangerous Exploration'

The noise the duct made when he landed on it was like a large boom and he froze as the two men turned to look directly at him!

Pyrra waited anxiously behind the building on the other end of the roof where she had banged the ducting with her tail. She was still very worried about Angus and not wanting to let her protector out of sight she took a chance and peered around the side of the building. The plan had worked and the two men walked cautiously in her direction but then she saw Angus dangling over the ducting. She could see he was still too high and hoped he was not going to let go as… 'Too late'!

Angus tried to run, but his legs had frozen solid in fear. The two large men now stared directly at him and he closed his eyes to wait on the inevitable trouble that would surely follow. He closed his eyes tight and wished he had listened Georgina.

"Now that was weird Ron" said one of the men.

"Yeah I could have sworn something hit that ducting" said the other.

"It was probably just heat inside the duct making the sheet metal react to the cold temperature on the outside" said the first man.

"Well hark at Albert Einstein here!" replied the other security man derisively.

"Leave it out!" snarled the man.

Another boom emanated from the direction Pyrra was hiding in, and both men spun around to face the source of the sound.

The green dragon had just witnessed the two men look directly at Angus. She had expected them to shout and run at the lad before they dragged him inside the building to Meredith, but nothing happened. Both men just stood calmly talking to each other as the lad stood too petrified to run. Pyrra thought hard about what to do next. 'I could just fly out and eat them' she thought but then made a face at such a repulsive thought. She had another look and since none of them had made any attempt to apprehend him she could only come to one conclusion. She looked at the lad closely and there was the answer staring her right in the face. Although she could still see him clear as day, he had somehow made himself invisible to the men! She realised the only way she could help him and flicked her tail against the metal of the ducting once again.

The booming sound forced Angus to open his eyes and he slowly looked in the direction of the two men expecting to be grabbed at any moment, but they were facing the opposite direction. He watched as they cautiously stepped towards the other building and Pyrra's hiding place. Seeing his chance Angus lightly jumped the remaining three feet to the ground and paused to ensure they had not heard him again. The men were now only a couple of metres away from the other doorway and he knew he had to act fast. He looked at the open doorway only a few steps away and could see that the two men had used a fire extinguisher to keep the door from closing and locking them on the roof. He thought about taking it away as he passed as that would stop them from following him and gain him a bit of time, but he also realised that might alert them to the presence of an intruder. Pyrra had given him just enough time to get down the fire escape stairway and as he tiptoed quietly down he turned back to see Pyrra flying off to the opposite side of the building just as the confused guards reached the spot where she had been hidden. He turned to climb down into the building, his heart pounding as he made every step of his descent. Angus did not understand why he had not been caught, but he knew that his good fortune would not last for long as the men would surely be following him down the staircase very soon.

Now he was inside the building, Angus found himself

wondering what to do next. In his mind the plan had been so simple. Sneak in and find the eggs. But now he was faced with a dilemma. Meredith had the top two floors and both of them encompassed the entire level of that building so he had too much ground to cover. He had to be careful trying to decide whether to go for the top floor or the one below. He was just about at the fire door to the top floor when he heard the guards battering the door shut above him as they replaced the extinguisher on its wall bracket. His heart rate raced as both men started to descend the stairs. Quickly he left the door and made his way further down the stairs as quickly and as quietly as he could. He tried to stay as close to the wall as possible to avoid being seen by the two guards.

"That was spooky Jeff" said the larger guard.

"Too right Ron" replied his friend.

"I've never heard those ducts make that kind of noise before" added the large man clearly phased by the episode above.

"Me neither… let's just keep it between us for now and get back to guarding her majesty's prized possessions!"

Angus never saw the nodded agreement from the guard called Ron, but he did now know where he had to go. He waited for the door to close behind the two men before he climbed the steps. The door had not quite shut fully and he placed his fingers tentatively into the gap to stop it. Both men had disappeared from sight and Angus, faced with no choice squeezed thought the doorway having barely opened it enough to allow his backpack to avoid being caught. He found himself in the middle of a long corridor with a brown wooden paneled door facing him. Reluctantly he poked his head out from the recessed fire escape doorway and he could see that the corridor led off to either side of his current position and that it had many similar doors to the one in front of him. 'Why do I get myself into these things?' he thought as he decided to go right towards the longer of the two sides. He decided to work his way systematically along the corridor and listen for sounds from inside the rooms before he had a look. This was really dangerous but if he got caught he would claim to be lost from one of the other floors and was just looking for his dad and bluff it out. It was a bit lame really but it was the best he could think of.

The first two doors were locked so he moved on to the next two. He moved as swiftly and silently as he could and at the third door he heard voices. He decided to leave that one as he could not see anything though the key hole. Glancing further along, he saw the lift for the building and noted the security camera opposite the lift doors. Clearly he could not go that way. One of the doors in the corridor was a very large double door and Angus guessed it would lead to a boardroom of some sort. Turning to the fourth door he listened intently and heard nothing, but just as his hand reached for the handle his attention was drawn to a noise from further up the corridor. Without thinking he grabbed the handle and tried to open the door. It was locked and as panic overcame his rational thoughts he ran to the next just as someone backed out from the large doorway. He desperately grabbed the handle and without bothering to check he sprang inside the room.

Luckily it was dark and empty. He had just enough sense to avoid slamming the door shut and left it slightly ajar. Angus tried to calm his breathing as his chest heaved due to the adrenalin that now pumped through his body. Now that he had a moment to consider what he had just seen, his thoughts filtered the information and began to make sense of it. The man backing out of the doorway seemed to be doing so in an apologetic manner. Angus had also heard a voice and at the time he was too panic-stricken to realise what his ears had picked up. Now he had to be sure and gathering his courage

he sneaked a look through the slither of doorway he had left open. He could hear someone apologising profusely about a failed experiment and then another voice rang out in the corridor. Angus heard the unmistakable tones of Meredith Quinton-Jones coming towards him.

"I expect results you fool as that is exactly what I am paying you for!" she bellowed at a little bald man in a white lab coat.

"Yes Madam, I will get you them, but you have to understand that this is not an exact science and we have no precedence to work by" replied the small man nervously.

Just remember that they are very precious and you had better look after them" she commanded.

Angus needed an improved viewpoint and risked opening the doorway a little further to adjust his view of the corridor. His heart literally jumped into his mouth as Meredith walked in his direction and appeared to be heading straight for the room he now hid in. Fortunately she was busy talking to the little man and had not seen him. Angus left the door and found a desk to hide under just as the pair reached the door. He held his breath until he heard the rattle of keys in the door opposite.

"Hurry up and unlock it!" she ordered.

Angus heard the lock turn and the door open just as a mobile rang.

"Yes…" said Meredith, "This is Meredith Quinton-Jones…" The young protector slid out from under the desk and slowly walked to the door.

"Yes hold on… I have to take this call in the office, you wait for me here" she snapped before striding back the way she had come.

Angus breathed a sigh of relief and watched the small man adjust his round glasses and make a face at her retreating back. He adjusted his lab coat and entered the opposite room. All the protector could do now was to sit tight until the coast was clear, but he knew one thing for sure. He needed to know what was in that room!

Angus pushed the door shut without fully closing it and took off his backpack. He looked at his surroundings and although the blinds were almost closed he still had enough light to see what was inside. He slid down the wall and searched for a chocolate bar he had stashed away in his backpack. As he munched on a chunk he noted the pictures on the walls all had a similar oil rig theme. They all depicted various types of large man made complicated looking structures. Some had flames spouting from pipes on the top of towers, others had ships moored alongside, and all of them had helicopter landing

pads. He had just munched the last square of chocolate when he heard the opposite door open. The small bespectacled man stood with a large steaming mug in his hand.

"Just who does she think she is? You wait for me here..." he muttered to himself as he mimicked her haughty voice, "I studied at Cambridge and she thinks she can talk to me like that..."

Angus watched him grumble all the way down the corridor and disappear into another room just before the lift. He seized his chance and glanced in both directions before he dived across the corridor. The lad grabbed the handle and turned it hopefully.

The door opened and he slipped inside the darkened room and leaned against the door whilst his eyes adjusted to the darkness. His hand brushed against the door knob on the inside and stopped against the key in the lock. He quickly spun and turned the key, locking it to ensure he was not discovered. He realised he could see the outline of the door because of a pale orange light. Turning slowly he tried to discover the source and his gaze was drawn to the middle of the room where it was brightest. He had just decided to take a look when the door knob rattled. He looked at the door and could hear the lab coat man muttering to himself again.

"Now where did I put that stupid key… she'll string me up when she gets back!"
Angus slowly backed away from the door as it rattled again.

"Hello! Who's in there?" he called loudly. "I'm going to get security and then you'll be in trouble!"
It went quiet but a few seconds later another voice appeared behind the door.

"And what makes you think someone is inside?" asked the deep voice of the guard Angus recognised as Jeff from the roof.

"Well it's locked from the inside… look you can see the key!" said the lab coat man.
The guard must have taken a few seconds to look and Angus chastised himself inwardly for not taking the key out of the door.

"Alright you've had your little joke, now open the door!" boomed the voice of the guard.
Angus tried to think of what to do next. How could he escape? All the time this had been going on he had slowly inched backwards and now had his back against a metal surface that was very hot. He turned and found that he was standing next to some sort of heater that stood on a frame with wheels. He

decided that since the guards already knew he was inside the room it would not be a problem if he switched on the light.

His eyes adjusted slowly and the glow from the middle of the room seemed to linger in front of his face for a few seconds as his brain caught up with what his eyes told it. He could see that the orange light glowed from the heat lamps and Angus edged closer to the source.

"OK we can see the lights are on so just open the door and we'll go easy on you!" shouted Jeff.

Angus ignored the pleas from outside the door and he pulled one of the metal frames aside to reveal what looked like a large glass dome, on the table, filled with straw. Angus had seen something like this before in his science lessons but this was much smaller; it was an incubator. Excitedly he looked for the socket that powered the lamps and switched them off before pushing them out of his way. He saw a pair of thick gloves on another table and quickly put them, still ignoring the commotion

outside the door. Tentatively he put his hand through one of the portholes and gently removed the straw on top. He grinned, as two perfect dragon eggs lay side-by-side, nestled in the warmth of the incubating box.

Chapter 24

'A Question of Balance'

Angus was overjoyed to have found the eggs, but now he had a problem; how on earth was he going to get them and indeed himself, out of the building? The banging at the door told him he was not going to leave that way and there was no other visible exit. He touched one of the eggs and was surprised to feel how warm it was even with the glove on. Suddenly it moved slightly…or was it just his imagination? Urged on by the increasingly desperate noise from behind the door he quickly examined the other egg. It appeared to be okay and both seemed in perfect condition

"I'm going to get the boss" said Ron the larger of the two guards.

Angus turned towards the door and realised he had better hurry things up as time was of the essence. He put his backpack on the floor and looked for something to wrap the warm eggs in. A thermal blanket lay folded on the table where he found the gloves, and he quickly used it to line the inside of his backpack. Gently he lifted the door of the incubator open and placed the eggs in the middle of the blanket and

tucked them in. He zipped up his bag and carefully hoisted it back onto his shoulders.

Angus was suddenly aware of someone else outside the door.

"What do you mean you can't get in?" asked a haughty voice. "Move aside!"

The young teenager looked around the room and realised it must have a window. He made for a heavy black curtain on the opposite wall to the door and pulled it aside. Light streamed in through the glass panes and he fumbled with the window catch as the door rattled.

"Open this door at once!" commanded Meredith. "Whoever you are believe me you will be in serious trouble if you do not open this door immediately!"

Ignoring this, Angus managed to pull the catch around and free the lock.

"You... brawn... kick in this door at once!" screamed Meredith angrily.

Inside the room Angus pulled very carefully at the sash window. He hoped it would slide upwards easily on its runners and not give away his escape route. It glided open and he closed the blackout curtains behind him to cover his tracks. With a loud crack that made him jump, the door fractured open in splinters. Meredith and the guards burst into the room with the nervous scientist scurrying behind them.

Angus cautiously lifted his left leg out through the window trying to feel for the ledge and most of all to keep calm. The afternoon sky was already darkening over the City. Bracing with his arms he lifted his right leg out and inched his body onto the wide ledge beyond. His heart thumped loudly in his chest as he strove not to be heard. He knew what he was doing was dangerous but he only hoped to gain some time until the coast was clear. Whoever had come into the room had now seen the empty incubator and Angus knew he only had moments until they checked the window. Carefully he turned and began to slowly slide the window down hoping it would not be heard. The sash moved noiselessly and Angus smiled as it reached the last few inches at the bottom. Suddenly the curtain flew back and Meredith, her face red with rage caught Angus as he pushed the window shut.

"YOU!" she screamed through the glass panes. "Just where do you think you're going, you little thief?" she raged.

The unexpected fright Meredith gave the young protector made him lose his balance and he wobbled backwards as he tried to regain his composure. He flailed for a few seconds as Meredith grabbed at the awkward mechanism of the window trying to get at him. Angus could see the guards eagerly grinning behind her as they realised they would now be called into action. After what seemed like an eternity the young protector regained his balance and grabbed the wall. Sensing his imminent capture he stood up and began to walk as quickly as he could along the ledge. The ledge that had seemed quite large to him before suddenly became very narrow as his mind told him just how much danger he was in. He dared not look down for fear of falling and he inched desperately away from the window.

In a fit of rage Meredith opened the sash wide and tried to grab the lad but by now he was well out of reach. The shrewd business woman quickly weighed up the situation and smiled cruelly.

"Where do you think you are going Angus?" she mocked. "We have you trapped and you have nowhere to go! If you jump, the eggs will be lost forever and neither of us wants that now do we?"

Angus wished that Pyrra was nearby as he was not sure how long he could evade capture on such a small ledge.

"I would rather let that happen than allow a witch like you get your hands on them!" he shouted defiantly turning towards

her.
The effort of shouting to her threw his balance and he flailed momentarily before he regained his grip on the stone surface.

"You're going to kill yourself you stupid boy… are those eggs really worth it?" she snarled at him. "You two go to the other windows and grab him!" she shouted back inside at the guards.
Before he knew it the window nearest him was opened to reveal the larger of the two men.

"C'mon son, give us the eggs" he said calmly.
Angus moved back the way he came and wondered where on earth Pyrra could be.

"Well don't just stand there, go out and get him!" screamed Meredith from the other window.
Angus inched back as the large man squeezed his huge body through the gap.

"I want danger pay for this" he growled at her, "this is not in my contract."

"Yes, yes… now just get him in here now!" she grinned malevolently.
The lad looked up towards the roof as he hoped to see his favourite green dragon appear to save the day but there was no sign of her. Then he

remembered Hedley and Latimer across on St Paul's and he turned to see if they were within range. Just as he did so he lost his footing and fell down only just catching his arms on the edge of the ledge. He dangled there desperately trying to get a foothold as the weight of the backpack pulled him away from the ledge. 'Where was Pyrra when he needed her?' he thought.

"Quickly, don't let the eggs fall…" screeched Meredith in desperation, "grab his backpack, don't worry about the boy!" Angus scrabbled frantically at the stonework just as the large guard made a grab for the top of his backpack. He missed and Angus watched as the top floor of the building began to drift away from him!

Chapter 25

'The Chase is On'

In slow motion Angus watched Meredith's face turn from anger into shock but he did not appear to be falling and for a second he thought he had the ability to fly. Then sound and motion returned and he could hear Meredith screaming above him as his body accelerated towards the ground.

Meanwhile Pyrra stood on the roof pacing up and down as she worried about the safety of her young protector.

"He'll be fine Pyrra… I'm sure of it!" said Wymarc in an attempt to calm her down.

"He's been in there fifteen minutes already" said Georgina equally concerned.

"I should never have allowed him to go…" she replied, "He is always getting into trou..."

The dragon stopped in mid sentence with a puzzled expression on her face.

"Whatever's the matter Pyrra?" asked Georgina, disturbed by the sudden silence.

The green dragon did not reply and instead took to the air and swept over the edge of the building.

Angus was free falling away from the top of the

building as he plummeted towards the pavement many floors below. He watched calmly as the top two floors passed him. The next thing he heard was the familiar beating of wings as Pyrra swooped underneath him and plucked him gently up to her chest.

"We appear to be making a habit of this!" she grinned at him as she swept up past the incredulous face of Meredith.

The guards looked at each other and then back to the point where Angus had just vanished.

"Tell me we just saw the lad disappear, Jeff" said the large guard on the ledge.

"We just saw him disappear, Ron" replied the other guard at the window.

"You two, get the rest of the men and make sure you have your Dragonore you imbeciles!" screamed Meredith from her window.

She slammed the window shut and turned to the small man in the lab coat.

"Did you see that?" she asked calmly.

"Y… yes" he replied quietly, "who'd of thought it. A l… live d… dragon here in the m… middle of London" he stammered as he fished a small glowing stone from his pocket and fingered it nervously.

"Of course there is you fool… in fact there are probably dozens of them!" she bellowed. "Now will your ideas work?"

"Work?" he replied clearly flustered. "Y… yes they will… but dragons…"

"Yes, yes… we've been over this… now, get out of my way you fool" she barked as she pushed him aside and strode purposefully from the room.

Meredith walked to the lift as she punched a number on her mobile.

"Get them ready… yes both of them… I'll be there in twenty minutes!" she barked before ending the call.

She walked into the lift, pressed the button for the ground floor and stood smirking as the doors closed in front of her.

Everything was going according to plan.

Pyrra flew up over the roof and back towards Wymarc and Georgina. She did not stop and carried on further to look for a safe place to land that was far enough away from Meredith and her henchmen. The other pair followed the green dragon across the river to alight in a large garden in front of the Tate Modern art gallery. Wymarc landed beside Pyrra just as Angus dropped from the green dragon's grip. He felt rather wobbly and tremendously grateful that his friend had managed

to catch him before he met with certain death. Georgina jumped down from Wymarc's back and ran to Angus.

"What happened?" she asked. "How did you get out and why were you in Pyrra's arms?"

Angus paused for breath and looked at Pyrra who knew he was grateful. She just smiled and nodded as he began to give an account of exactly what happened.

"Angus you idiot... you could have been killed" Georgina admonished him.

The lad just smiled and took off his backpack. Up until that point he had not told them that he had managed to retrieve the eggs.

"Well it was worth it to get these!" he said, triumphantly displaying the precious cargo inside the thermal blanket.

Georgina just squealed in delight and threw her arms around him giving him a big kiss at the same time. He immediately went red with embarrassment and Pyrra laughed. 'What a lad' she thought, 'He could jump into the jaws of death at the drop of a hat but give him a girl to deal with and he falls to bits.'

"Good work young man, but how did you know he was in trouble Pyrra?" asked Wymarc after Georgina finally let him go.

"He called to me" she replied softly looking into the lad's confused face.

"He did? But why didn't we hear him?" asked Georgina equally confused.

"Because he used his mind to call me" she replied matter-of-factly.

"How could he do that?" asked Georgina looking at him strangely.

"That's a good question… perhaps we should ask him" replied the green dragon.

Angus felt all eyes were on him and he began to think about some of the strange things he had managed to do over the last few months. The only thing he could think of was that he managed to find or draw some power from the Dragonore whenever he needed it. This was usually when he was in desperate trouble, but how could he explain this to the others without sounding crazy?

"I don't know… it just happens… I needed Pyrra and somehow she knew it" he said smiling at her.

"Yes and I'm glad I was in tune as that was a bit too close for comfort!" added Pyrra.

"But at least I got the eggs!" said Angus holding one of them up.

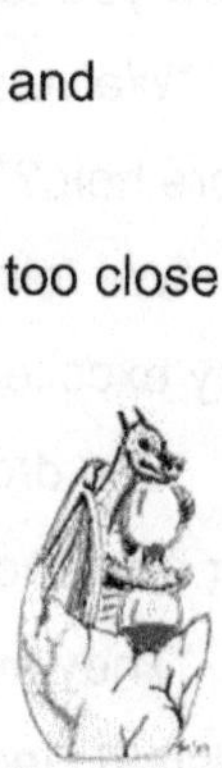

"I think we left behind a lot of annoyed humans in Halcyon House and I don't think it will be long before that woman comes after us" said Georgina looking at the Millennium Bridge and St Paul's Cathedral dominating the skyline behind it.

Angus knew she was right and they needed a plan, but he took the time to stroke Pyrra's nose. The bond between them was stronger now than ever, but he was still amazed that he had managed to summon her without sound.

Latimer and Hedley landed softly beside them, but instead of entering into their usual rhetoric they spoke in more serious tones.

"Finally we've caught up with you!" shouted Hedley.

"We saw what was happening and went to get Faris" said Latimer.

"He called the others to Smithfield and he has a plan to allow you to escape" added Hedley.

"We've already escaped... Why would he think we needed more help?" asked Georgina confused.

"We followed that woman after your hasty exit... Oh by the way excellent catch lovey" said Hedley to Pyrra.

"She drove to a heliport near here and met some more of her men" added Latimer.

"They had guns and they're searching for you now!" finished Hedley.

"Guns?" squealed Georgina, "What are we going to do?" Angus hugged the backpack gently to his chest so as not to damage the precious contents. This was getting serious and he racked his brains trying to think of what to do next.

"You said Faris had a plan?" he asked seriously.

"Yes dearie, you need to follow us to the Palace" replied Latimer.

"The Palace… you mean Buckingham Palace?" gasped Georgina.

"Yes lovey, they can't fly in that area and you'll be safe" added Hedley.

The protectors wasted no more time and jumped up onto the

backs of Pyrra and Wymarc. That was when both dragons first sensed a problem. Angus watched the green dragons sensitive ears twitch as she looked across the river. Soon both protectors could hear the roaring sound of two helicopters as they swept over the building and across the darkening sky. A tremendous whipping wind pushed down on them as both helicopters hovered directly above them.

Luckily there were too many trees to allow the

helicopters to land in Bankside Gardens, but it did mean that Meredith was on to them already. The dragons and protectors did not move, and the few art lovers still visiting the Gallery stood gawping at the black and red helicopters as their side doors slid open. Two men in each of the cabins appeared on the edge of the doorway holding rifles which panicked the visitors and sent them running and screaming away from the scene, but it was dragons they were after and Angus shouted at Pyrra to move fast and get airborne quickly.

"But surely they can't see us?" shouted Wymarc.

The dragons began to take off in great haste when the men fired the first shots.

"Yes they…" began Latimer in reply, but he did not finish and Angus turned to see the slate coloured dragon collapse on the ground mid sentence.

Chapter 26

'Divide to Conquer'

Staying low and avoiding the rotor blades of the helicopters, the other three dragons followed the River Thames upstream in the direction of Buckingham Palace. The agile helicopters started to give chase; both pilots finding it hard to believe that Meredith had been right all along and dragons really did exist. Like most of her employees they had privately thought their boss a little crazy in the head, but lured by the promise of extra cash they did as they were instructed and with the benefit of Dragonore, now they could see their prey.

"Angus they're shooting at us!" screamed Georgina.
The lad turned to see Meredith herself sitting in the front of one of the helicopters urging the pilots to fly closer. Blackfriars Railway Bridge loomed in front of them and Angus remembered that the road bridge ran parallel, just on the other side. They were very close together and he hoped to buy them some time.

"Pyrra, fly under the bridge and then stop" he shouted.
The green dragon groaned and missed a beat of her wings. Two darts had ripped into the

membranes of her right wing and as a result of this she dipped a few feet towards the water. Pyrra juddered momentarily before regaining her rhythm and Angus reached down to pull a bright orange shaft from her wing.

"It's a knock out dart!" he said leaning forward.

The green dragon sighed and with a determined look on her face pushed for the bridge in a zig-zag motion to throw off their aim.

"Don't worry they didn't hit my body, only my wing!" she shouted back.

They dipped under the steel girders and Angus watched as the black and red helicopters swept upwards to avoid a collision with the bridge.

"STOP!" he shouted at the top of his voice.

The dragons pulled up immediately and hovered as close to the underside of the bridge as they could, Angus hoped the steel girders would block any potential attack and give them time to think.

"We haven't got long before they work out where we are but I have a plan, listen up…" shouted Angus to the others.

He began to explain what he wanted them to do before Meredith realised she had been duped.

The two pilots swept the helicopters over the top of the

bridge and only just missed a train on the tracks. The radios in the cockpit crackled with noisy chatter as word filtered around the authorities that two helicopters had fired rifles into the gardens near the Tate. The pilot in the lead helicopter looked at Meredith.

"Ignore it!" she said, "I've got the perfect alibi for this little stunt and the Police won't bother us" she finished.
The pilot forced the joystick forward and sped to the other side of Blackfriars Bridge watching for the emergence of the dragons, but they did not appear.

"Turn around!" shouted Meredith angrily.
He did as he was told and spun the aircraft to face the way they had come.

"Where are they?" she bellowed.

"They must have stopped" replied the pilot.

"Order him to go back to the other side... quickly!" she shouted at the flustered man.
He started to relay the message through his head set to the pilot in the other helicopter.

Finished with his explanation of the plan Angus looked to the others for feedback. Georgina looked pensive; Wymarc showed no hint of emotion; Pyrra winked to confirm she was okay and poor Hedley stared in the direction of the prone body of Latimer.

"He'll be fine once you reach the others and come back for him..." said the young lad sympathising with the dragon, "Are we all ready then?"

They all nodded their affirmation.

Meredith watched as a blue dragon carrying the young girl sped off back in the direction they had just come from. Another dragon she did not recognise flew from under the road bridge and straight between the two aircraft as they hovered above the Thames. Pyrra shot out from between the two bridges and followed the road south, away from Blackfriars Station giving the pilots the unenviable task of choosing which dragon to follow. As the helicopters wavered uncertainly, Meredith, a business woman much more used to making executive decisions, barked out orders to the pilots.

"Tell that idiot to follow the blue dragon and *you*, follow the green one!"

The noses of both aircraft dipped sharply as they began a high speed chase of the dragons over the darkening streets of London.

Angus realised that Georgina had a bag with her and he hoped she might be able to create a plausible decoy. So far it appeared to have worked as one of the pilots flew after her and Wymarc, allowing Hedley to get help from the City Guardians. Pyrra used the streets as cover to avoid Meredith's pursuit, the green dragon skimming as close to the cars and buses as she could. The helicopter could not fly too low and this made her a much harder target to hit. She flicked right at the next junction and this threw the pilot, as he did not expect her sharp turn. He jerked the joystick and banked too hard almost throwing one of the men from the belly of the aircraft. The marksman dangled precariously from his safety line as one of the other men tried to pull him back inside. Pyrra had them confused now and she sped up another street and down an alley.

"That should shake them off!" shouted Pyrra in triumph. As they passed the Oxo Tower, Angus spun around because he heard the sound of the helicopter behind him and was dismayed to see the black and red aircraft still in hot pursuit.

Georgina and Wymarc had set off in the other direction along the river; passing under London Bridge. The blue dragon was enjoying the adventure and using dragon time he flew at high speed through the middle of Tower Bridge. Georgina turned to look back and was aghast to see that the helicopter still doggedly tailed them so they had not managed to out fly

them yet. Wymarc did not follow the ox bow curve of the Thames but cut straight across towards the Docklands. Darts whizzed past them as the dragon swerved left and right in an attempt to evade being hit. Georgina spotted some taller buildings further on and called to Wymarc to head for them.

Faris paced up and down, the other Guardians waiting with him in the grounds of Buckingham Palace. He was just thinking of sending out search parties when Hedley skidded into the middle of them. The dragon managed to blurt out what had happened and where Pyrra and Wymarc were going.

"You two go with Hedley to get Latimer and take him somewhere safe" he commanded Lyell and Fulbert. "Wulfric, you're with me. The rest of you go to find Wymarc and knock that machine out of our sky!"

The orders given, eight dragons sprang into the air.

For five full minutes the blue body of Wymarc dodged and weaved through Canary Wharf in an attempt to avoid the darts aimed in his direction. One of them hung perilously close to the knuckle joint in his right wing; while his left wing had a rupture in one of the membranes. The tear hampered his flying and it was only the distance the helicopter had to maintain due to the taller buildings that saved him from further damage. Georgina was really worried about Wymarc as he struggled to maintain his level with an injured wing. She hoped they could outlast the helicopter, but it was only when they past a tall silvery building that she spotted the distinctive white roof of the Dome across the river.

"Can you make it over there?" she asked.

Wymarc answered by dipping his head and diving forward as fast as he could go. The blue dragon had gained an advantage in distance as the tall building blocked the vision of the pilot. He pointed the aircraft in the direction of the Dome and gave chase.

Dhruv, Lothair and Kennard had gained height and used their keen vision to look for Wymarc and Georgina. They had been searching for sometime before Lothair growled and indicated the helicopter's flashing lights below them. The three dragons could see that Wymarc was trying to make it to the large white Dome and they dove like a jet fighter squadron homing in on a target.

The Dome's lighting made it a spectacular sight against the late afternoon skyline of London. The spikes that supported the roof glowed in the darkness topped with their red warning lights. Georgina urged the dragon onward but she could hear the noise of the aircraft closing in on them and was not sure they

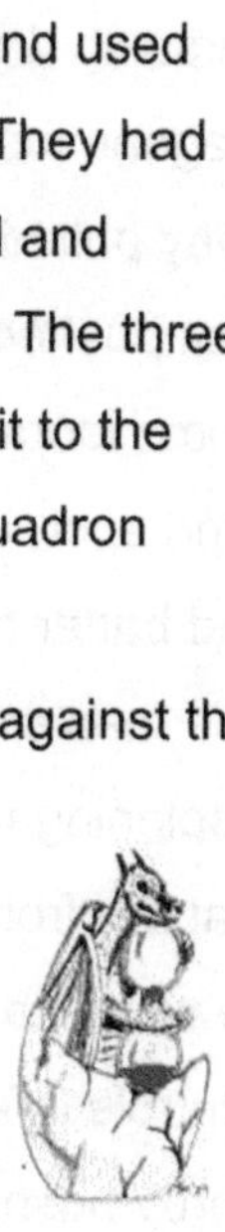

would make it. Suddenly she heard a roar and spinning around she witnessed three of the City Guardians drop from the sky like fighter pilots from the Second World War, as they swarmed around the unsuspecting pilot. Having received the shock of his life the poor man had pulled the aircraft sideways in an evasive maneuver. The water in the river sprayed upwards as he came too close to hitting the surface. This diversion gave Wymarc enough time to get to the Dome, flying between two of the twelve towering frames that held the roof up. The pilot quickly regained control and the men inside the cabin fired wildly at the pursuing dragons. Now the tables had turned as the three dragons took it in turns to attack the underside of the aircraft. They pulled and rammed it with all of their strength but still the pilot pushed the black and red machine towards his target. The Dome loomed in front of the attackers just as Dhruv found a blind spot. Unseen he managed to grab the side of the aircraft and batter his armored forehead into the pilot's side window. The man screamed as he lost control of the helicopter sending it spinning towards the roof. The pilot now saw the many cables that ran from the top of each tower to the domed surface and he was heading straight for them. Instinctively he pulled on the controls to avoid a disaster of massive proportions just as Dhruv pushed away to safety. To the pilot's credit he managed to divert the aircraft away from the modern icon, but he only succeeded in ditching into the Thames. Georgina watched as the helicopter sank under the murky surface, but she was relieved to the men escape unharmed. The trio scrambled from the water only to be grabbed by the security force that patrolled the Dome's perimeter.

All four dragons met on the far side of the great structure and rested for a few moments on the famous curved roof of London's millennium landmark safe in the knowledge they had avoided capture. Georgina smiled at the blue dragon and patted his scaly nose. She had met her match in Wymarc and he was as much of an adventure seeker as she was. The young girl was still concerned for the others, but Wymarc was unable to help Pyrra now and she fervently hoped that both the dragon and Angus were as fortunate as they themselves had been.

Chapter 27

'Special Effects'

Meanwhile a police boat, with blue lights flashing, sped after the low flying helicopter, unaware of the target the aircraft followed. Pyrra used the ships as blockers as she swept around them. Angus smiled, as he knew it would only be a matter of time before a police helicopter would be sent to chase the villains across the London sky. Inside the cockpit Meredith told the pilot to ignore the summoning calls from the authorities on the radio and instead she dialed her mobile phone.

"Have you spoken to them yet?" she asked someone on the other end of the line. "Do it now!" she shouted before ending the call.

She grinned triumphantly and pointed towards the green dragon that weaved in front of them.

"Now get me that dragon!" she growled.

Pyrra swooped low under Waterloo Bridge and Angus nearly got his feet wet as they skimmed the River Thames. The young protector hoped the police would come to their rescue and was relieved to see them chase the rogue helicopter up river until they had cleared the bridge, but instead of continuing the pursuit they suddenly turned the police boat away. Angus watched in dismay as the blue lights went out at the same time the siren lamely died.

"If you don't mind me asking Miss, how did you manage that?" asked the pilot clearly impressed.

"Oh that was easy..." she replied looking smug, "you just need friends in the correct places and in this case it's a film producer and we are filming for him!"

In front of the helicopter, Pyrra flew at great speed to the Royal Festival Hall and swooped through the place spinning pedestrians as she past. No one knew what had caused the wind until the helicopter appeared and they gestured angrily at the noisy aircraft. By this time the green dragon was tiring and Angus knew she would need to rest before long. A large office block gave them some respite forcing the pilot upwards and away from Pyrra giving her time to fly around and down a busy street. When they cleared the building again Angus saw the London Eye all lit up, which he thought was way cooler than any ferris wheel he had ever seen. He had heard that it never stopped moving and passengers had to jump on and off the scenic ride in motion. The little glass capsules allowed for a magnificent and unrivalled scenic view of London. Well, only if you did not know any dragons! He really wanted to ride it one

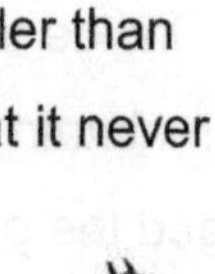

day, but it would probably never be as good as the views he had now. He could see the queues of people as they waited for their turn and he hoped Pyrra would be able to use it as another way to evade their pursuers.

Meredith appeared behind them again and the darts began to fly past. Pyrra banked right and something whizzed past Angus' head. He stared in horror as one of the darts had stuck in one of her horns. That was too close for comfort and he hoped she could keep it up. Suddenly two objects sped past them, one on either side of her wings. Angus turned to see a spout of flame billow onto the windscreen of the helicopter as Faris tried to allow Pyrra time to escape.

"Get out of here!" he bellowed as both he and Wulfric grappled with the underside of the aircraft.

Angus watched as it spun out of control directly in front of the London Eye.

Inside the cockpit Meredith raged at the pilot ordering him to maintain control. She knew what was going on and she urged the pilot to shake the dragons off and catch up with the lad.

"I want that bag and I will triple your pay if you help me capture it!" she encouraged.

Any of the tourists who were taking pictures of the splendid nighttime views would have been amazed if they had realised dragons were swooping in and out of their snapshots! Now instead of trying to get the best photos of famous London landmarks below them like the Post Office Tower, St Paul's cathedral in the distance, Buckingham Palace and of course the Houses of Parliament on the opposite side of the river bank; they craned their necks to take pictures of the crazy pilot in the red and black helicopter. The sightseers were rather alarmed by the erratic flight of the aircraft, which was a bit too close to the Eye for safety.

"Wonderful special effects with the flames... Must be some movie!" said one man to his wife.

"What, this close to the Eye?" she asked, "Don't be daft Bert" she added as she carried on taking photographs of the view.

Unbeknown to the sightseers who of course could not see the dragons, the helicopter was constantly being buzzed by two of the City Guardians and Faris was enjoying the fun.

Westminster Bridge loomed in front of the escaping pair and Angus had an idea when he saw what was behind it.

"We're right next to the Houses of Parliament..." he shouted, "Fly around the back of it and then we can use it as cover once we're out of sight. We should be able to hide easily enough amongst the turrets and towers!"

Pyrra dipped under the bridge and kept to the shadows created by the powerful lights around the famous building. Angus hoped it would stop Meredith from seeing exactly where they went and allow them to slip away. He hoped Georgina and Wymarc were doing much better against the other helicopter.

In the helicopter Meredith had her sights firmly set on Angus and his backpack, but somehow she lost him in the lights of Westminster.

"Get rid of these dragons and find the boy!" she screamed at the poor pilot.

The flustered man was being harassed by dragons on the outside and a dragon on the inside of the helicopter, but somehow he managed to shake off Faris and Wulfric and head up river past Big Ben. The green dragon watched them go, safely hidden in one of the darkest corners of the Parliament buildings roof.

"Are you okay?" asked Angus reaching up to pull the dart from her horn.

"That was a close one" she chuckled.

"Yeah, too close!" agreed Angus smiling at her.

Faris suddenly landed beside them causing Angus to jump.

"They've gone, and Wulfric is tailing them to make sure they don't come back" he said.

"Good and thank you for helping" said Pyrra looking very tired.

"You're welcome!" replied Faris smiling.

"Did anyone go to help the others?" asked Angus urgently.

"I sent three and I'm sure she will be fine, as will Latimer" replied Faris confidently.

The teenage lad wished he could share the black dragon's faith but he would only be satisfied when they were all safe at Calmor with the eggs. He immediately grabbed his bag and unzipped it. The two pearlescent ovals were still warm, although he could touch them with his bare hands now.

"They've cooled down a little. Will they still be okay?" he asked Pyrra, concern in his voice.

"They'll be fine… Lay them on the roof and stand back" she replied.

Angus quickly did as he was told, unwrapping them from the thermal blanket and laying them gently on the roof tiles. The dragon inhaled deeply and blew a concentrated flame onto the eggs bathing them in heat. Angus watched in awe as

they glowed red, changed to yellow and then white hot, forcing him to shield his eyes. The best bit was yet to come as the warm shells appeared to turn translucent revealing the Fire Whelps within. Pyrra stopped breathing fire and the three of them watched in awe as the silhouetted baby dragons wriggled inside their shells as if doing some sort of dance to inaudible

music. The heat began to disperse and the shells started to return to their normal colour again. Angus blinked with red spots in front of his eyes and looked at Pyrra; it was the most wonderful thing he had ever seen! She smiled at him before she picked them up and placed them back inside the thermal blanket. Angus zipped up the bag and threw it over his shoulder feeling the warmth of the eggs within; just as the wind picked up.

Wulfric tracked the helicopter almost all the way to Heathrow airport before he lost it. The sky became congested with air traffic of various types and the brown dragon became confused as to where his target was. After one last look he decided to head home, satisfied he had seen the attackers off. Using dragon time he pushed back into the heart of London to Westminster. The city flashed past beneath him and Wulfric felt more alive now than he had done for many years. In the distance his keen eyesight was drawn to a bright flame on the roof of the Parliament building and he guessed that was where he would find Faris and the others. It was just when he approached the building that the first dart found its target in his shoulder. By the time he realised it the second, third and fourth darts had hit his back and the roof disappeared in a blur as he lost consciousness.

Angus saw the body of Wulfric spin through the air as he tumbled towards the roof. Faris was first to react as he jumped into the air and tried to catch his friend. The momentum of the falling dragon was too much and the leader of the City

Guardians was pushed backwards into the famous clock tower of Big Ben. The two dragons fell to the roof below, forcing Angus and Pyrra to take evasive action. The young protector rolled sideways to avoid the limp body of Wulfric and somehow managed to twist his body to avoid rolling onto the eggs. He looked up to see the first darts hit the roof in front of his face.

"They're on to us" shouted Pyrra as she stretched her wings for take off.

The young protector did not need to be told twice and like a sprinter coming out of the blocks he vaulted forward and jumped up onto her back just as she sprung into the air. All of this took place in seconds and the marksmen in the helicopter fired repeatedly at her green body in an effort to bring her down.

Darts flew past them and Pyrra wheeled sideways in an effort to dodge this latest onslaught. They were sitting ducks but somehow she managed to confuse the marksmen by slipping in and out of dragon time. She flew around the tall clock tower that had been an iconic symbol of London for 150 years in an effort to avoid her attackers. The pilot maneuvered the aircraft with great skill and as she rose in height he spiraled upward having anticipated her next move. Pyrra flicked her wings and flew very close to the south face of Big Ben when the helicopter suddenly appeared in front of her. The pilot

dipped the nose forward and the rotor blades forced the dragon backwards. To avoid having her head cut off Pyrra crashed back into the white face of the clock smashing some of the stained glass panes.

Chapter 28

'In the Face of Time'

Angus was almost crushed and saw his only chance for safety was to jump for the clock face. Despite the height he did not hesitate for a second as he grabbed for something to hold onto, and the nearest thing was the minute hand. At that moment Faris attacked the underside of the helicopter and pulled it back away from Pyrra. The black dragon flailed as it spun out of control and almost hit the tower, but somehow he managed to continue to snap at the cockpit window. The pilot screamed incoherently as his vision was filled with a full set of very sharp teeth.

"Get this thing under control before you kill us all!" shouted Meredith unsympathetically at him.

Pyrra dropped towards the pavement below then regained her composure and flew off in the direction of the London Eye. Angus thought she had not realised he had been separated from her. When he saw the helicopter finally free itself from Faris and give chase, he knew what he had to do. Apparently no one had seen him on the clock face and taking stock of his predicament, he slid down the big hand towards the middle of the clock. He felt a little safer there, and luckily he was used to heights, but he was still exposed on the open clock face and he steadied himself to look for a way inside the clock face. The broken panes did not appeal as they had too many sharp edges but he spied a little maintenance door in the face of the clock and somehow he managed to slide down the hour hand to get to it. The whole time he did this he did not stop to think about any sightseers below who might be taking pictures of the crazy boy on the face of Big Ben. He was able to open the small door and he gratefully crawled inside. Normally it would be big enough for him to squeeze into, but because of his backpack and the bulky eggs he struggled. Now unsure of their safety, he pulled the backpack open and peered in. The radiating warmth of the eggs hit his face and he could feel the vibrations as the Fire Whelps wriggled inside. They were safe for now and he thought it best if he stayed hidden and wait for Pyrra to shake off the helicopter and hopefully come back for him.

Meredith and the pilot had not noticed that the green dragon was now flying solo. Pyrra pushed hard as she tried to lose the helicopter and find a way back to Angus. She could sense he was temporarily safe, but that would not last long and somehow she had to find a way of knocking this crazed

human from the sky. She used the bridges to stop Meredith's men from getting a decent aim, but despite her best attempts, darts flew inches past her body. By using dragon time effectively she managed to draw them well away from Big Ben before they noticed the absence of a rider.

"Where's the boy?" bellowed Meredith at the pilot.
The woman, angered by the thought of losing the eggs, replayed the last few minutes and instructed the pilot to fly straight at Big Ben.

Angus watched the dragon draw the helicopter away from his rather precarious viewing point. Luckily some one had seen him crawl inside, and before he knew it, Faris hovered in front of him.

"Anything I can do?" asked the black dragon with a grin.
The lad's view of Pyrra was obscured now, but he knew she was tiring and he thought about what they could do to draw the attackers away. He smiled and pushed his backpack out towards the leader of the City Guardians.

"Can you take this and keep it from them?" asked Angus smiling.

"It will be a pleasure!" shouted Faris.
He took the backpack from Angus in full view of the helicopter as it returned to the clock tower.

Pyrra realised the ploy had not worked and seeing the aircraft turn back towards Big Ben, she attacked. Before the pilot knew it he was fighting to control the helicopter as the green dragon wrestled with the under carriage.

"Get her off before she brings us down!" he growled at the marksmen.

One of the men dropped outside the doorway, his harness the only thing that kept him from falling as he spun in the air. Pyrra could see he was having trouble getting a shot, but she also knew it was only a matter of time before she was hit with one of those darts. She looked up and saw Faris had found Angus and satisfied he was saved, she let go just as the first dart hit her.

Angus watched the black dragon slowly peel away with the backpack in full sight of Meredith. He turned his attention to Pyrra and realised she was in grave danger as a marksman dangling outside the helicopter managed to shoot at her. Pyrra tried to dodge away from the aircraft, but the sniper appeared to shoot several darts at her body and from where Angus was sitting, they all hit the target. He watched in silent horror as his best friend now flew unsteadily in his direction. She looked groggy and lurched sideways from the effects of the sleeping

darts. Suddenly she started to spin out of control and Angus feared for her life as she spiraled out of sight.

The helicopter, now free of the green dragon flew after Faris at full throttle. He had a good head start, but they tried to keep up with the wily dragon who, having the advantage of dragon time, was gaining distance with the backpack in his fore claws.

Distressed, Angus tried to think but his mind was clouded with images of his friend lying on the ground badly injured or worse. He did not know how he was going to get out from the clock face as he was now abandoned!

Chapter 29

'Alone in the Dark'

"Why the long face?" said a voice from outside the clock. The young protector turned to see a familiar cheeky green scaly face before him and he had never been so pleased to see her.

"Pyrra!" he shouted. "But I saw you shot by at least four darts!"

"Yes they do sting when they hit but they don't stun you immediately and I was able to swipe them out as I barrel rolled downwards!" she replied whilst brandishing four bright orange darts.

"But… I… thought…" stammered Angus, and then he just grinned, "Cool!"

"I thought so too… Admittedly I am a bit groggy, but it was mostly play acting" she added by way of explanation and looking quite proud of herself.

Pyrra's great wings wafted slowly, keeping her perfectly poised in front of the clock face and he carefully lifted his hoodie with its precious cargo, out to her and climbed on her back.

"So what's the plan?" asked Pyrra over her

shoulder.

"We've to meet at the eye of the serpent" said Angus mysteriously.

"Oh very secretive… so where is that?" enquired the dragon further.

"Hyde Park… Faris said the others would meet us there" replied Angus. "That's where they meet when they have trouble!"

"So they don't give their hiding places away… Makes sense" said Pyrra.

They flew away from the clock face not a moment too soon as Big Ben was just about to launch into its world famous chimes. The boy and dragon would surely have been deafened at such close range!

Ten minutes later using a dragon time journey to Hyde Park both Angus and Pyrra appeared from the dark clouds.

"So what exactly is the eye of the serpent?" asked Pyrra as the cloud thinned around them.

"All Faris said was we would know it when we saw it from above" replied Angus as he looked down.

Pyrra looked down and could see no serpent eyes in the park but Angus just smiled.

"There… Can't you see it?" he pointed.

Pyrra squinted as she tried to see what Angus obviously could.

"Look at the long lake and follow it onto the pathways at this end" he explained. "The pathways form the head..."

"And the eye at that end" she finished for him tilting her head to one side.

Spiraling downwards towards the serpent eye they could now see that the others were already waiting in the shadowy trees nearest the eye and Angus was glad to see Latimer appeared to be alive and well. Soon they were laughing and chatting as they relived their adventures in the rose garden of Hyde Park at the Buckingham Palace end of Serpentine Lake. Georgina counted the City Guardians but she could only see eight instead of the full compliment of nine. Angus had noticed this also and was worried about Faris who had not been seen since he flew off with the backpack.

"How are the eggs Pyrra?" asked Angus.

The dragon looked at the wrapped up hoodie in her fore claws and laying it gently on the ground, unwrapped the precious package. Everyone gathered around to gaze at the pearlescent eggs, looks of awe on every dragon face. Suddenly there was an almighty crash through the braches of the nearest tree and Faris appeared in a heap of twigs and broken

branches.

His back was punctured by stun darts and he looked exhausted, but he still carried the backpack. The dragons immediately surrounded him, concerned for his well-being.

"I… I'm fi… fine" he assured them, "J… just a little groggy…" he added waving them away impatiently.

The leader of the City Guardians stood up; wobbled a couple of steps sideways and then fell forward onto the grass.

"Let's just sit you down here for a few minutes" said Pyrra gently helping him sit up and removing the three darts from the middle of his back. It was amazing he had managed to stay conscious with so many sleeping darts in his hide, but he was tough enough to have defeated Felspar so a few darts were not going to stop him.

"Thanks for helping get rid of Meredith" said Angus gently taking the backpack from Faris.

"M… my pleasure a… Angus" replied the black dragon as he tried to focus on the protector.

Angus gently opened the backpack and put the eggs inside, but he could not help checking the precious contents again. He examined them closely and miraculously they were still intact and just as importantly, still warm. He could feel throbbing from one of the eggs and then the noise grew louder and gradually the sound of a helicopter overhead made him look up. Apparently Faris had not lost the pursuers and they certainly had not given up. Angus knew they had to get the eggs away very quickly, but he needed time to think if they were ever going to get them back to Rhys before they hatched. He looked at his watch, it would be close, but they should still be able to make it if they moved quickly; and he knew dragons were good at that.

"Pyrra, Natural History Museum, quick!" he shouted as he sprang up onto her back. "The rest of you scatter!"

"We're going with him" shouted Georgina at Wymarc. The City Guardians reluctantly abandoned their wounded leader and dispersed like a flock of birds startled by a stalking cat.

The helicopter pilot tried desperately to maintain control of the aircraft and to go after the correct dragon whilst Meredith screamed at him.

"That one you fool… NO… the other one… The other one you idiot, there, can't you see the boy?"

The tactic worked and both Pyrra and Wymarc were able to get some distance between them and the pursuers before the chase began again.

They only had a short distance to travel

westwards across the early evening sky over Knightsbridge and Pyrra landed near the entrance of the Natural History Museum and both riders dismounted.

"Pyrra I need you to go and sit on the roof with Wymarc" he said.

"But they'll see me!" she replied, astonished at his request.

"That's the idea" he replied darkly. "Trust me, it'll be fine!" Georgina looked up at the Victorian animal sculptures illuminated in the late afternoon darkness of winter and found them quite creepy. It was as if every stone beast seemed to be staring at them. Angus wasted no time in finding the entrance and made his way inside the building as one of the last admissions of the day, with Georgina following close behind. The two dragons flew onto the roof as instructed and it was not long before Meredith and her men arrived.

Inside the building the two protectors made their way through the crowd as quickly as they could. There were not so many visitors as yesterday and they made their way quickly through the halls to the dinosaur section. Angus suddenly pulled Georgina aside and they ducked behind one of the scenes surrounding the exhibits. It was near to closing time again and soon the noise of the visitors petered out.

"What are we doing here Angus?" whispered Georgina with

great concern.
She had followed him blindly, such was her trust in him, but without any clue as to what plan her friend had in mind she was now a little worried.

"I have a plan that should get Meredith out of the way for good" he replied softly, "assuming it works."

"Assuming it works! What do you mean assuming it works?" Angus paid no attention to her as he heard the familiar tannoy announcement for all visitors to leave the building. He hoped that Meredith and her men had also managed to get into the building before closing time. All they had to do now was wait.

They sat quietly on the floor for some time and Angus glanced at his watch. It was now after seven o'clock and they had been sitting for almost two hours.

"Here, keep this safe" he said to Georgina as he removed his backpack.

"Where are you going?" she asked with concern.

"I'm just going to take a quick look… don't worry, I'll be back before you know it" he added in reply to the look on her face.
He stood up and slipped from their hiding place and carefully made his way back towards the main entrance.

Meredith and two of her men were now inside the building hidden behind a doorway as they too waited for the lights to go out. The three of them stood in a cupboard, which had been locked until one of her men had picked the lock. She had no wish to know how he had learnt such a skill, but needless to say it was probably not in any institution she was likely to visit. Her face showed no emotion whatsoever as she watched the door and when the light from under the door went out she grimaced as she opened it. The museum was now pitch black.

The sudden darkness caused Angus to freeze where he stood. His heart rate rose and began pounding in his ears as his mind sought to adjust to the lack of light. What had been complete darkness now started to form shapes as his eyes caught up and the shadowy world that formed around him became scarier by the second. The model animals and skeletons that entertained visitors during the daylight were now transformed into hideous shapes, promising doom. All of this passed through the mind of the young protector and as always he was able to capture his fears, storing them deep inside to give himself strength. A door opened up ahead and he ducked behind a particularly fearsome bear that had appeared quite harmless in the daytime. Three figures flitted through the passageway and he heard a very familiar voice command the men to search in different directions. One of the men crept past his hiding place and Angus was glad he was safely tucked into the space behind the bear. At least now he knew the plan was working and all he had to do now was get back to Georgina.

The young girl was frantic with worry in the darkness and where on earth was Angus? Why she had let him talk her into this she never knew. At the start of the day she had been absolutely determined not to let him go off on one of his adventures without her and now look where she was; right in the thick of it with him! Admittedly she could see how easy it was to get embroiled in an adventure when things happened so fast, but she had hoped to bring some sense to this trip and instead Angus had led the way throughout. She resolved to have a few words with him when they got back assuming they did get back, of course.

"Hi" said Angus as he jumped in behind the screen.

"Angus… you scared the life out of me!" she hissed slapping his arm at the same time.

"Sorry" he replied rubbing his arm and thinking this was becoming a habit of hers. "They're here and I need to do something. Wait here!" Before she could utter a protest he was gone again, this time with the backpack. Making sure

there was no one around, Angus vaulted over the rail that was there to keep the public off the exhibits. Georgina watched in horror as he removed two of the dinosaur eggs from the model nest and carefully placed the dragon eggs in the vacant spaces amongst the remaining model dinosaur eggs.

"What on earth are you doing?" she asked when he returned.

"Don't worry, they'll be safe there for now" he reassured her.

He opened his backpack and showed her the two model eggs wrapped in his hoodie. He handed her the thermal blanket and was just about to say something when they heard a sound. They risked a peek from behind the scenery and saw one of the Meredith's men as he crept through the dinosaur section of the museum. A shaft of light lit the man's face and Angus recognised him as Jeff, one of the men from the roof of Halcyon House. Neither of the protectors dared breathe as he stood next to the exhibit with the nest and stared directly at the eggs. Angus thought he had blown it, but instead of bending to pick up the eggs, Jeff moved on into the next area.

Both protectors let out a collective sigh of relief as they watched the man go.

"Okay, you keep the blanket with you as I hope we will

need it later. I'm going to take these and go find Meredith" said the lad turning to Georgina.

"What happens next?" she asked.

"I don't know, but you need to stay with the eggs and keep an eye on them" he replied in total honesty "I think they're safer here."

Before she could argue he was gone and she was now alone and quite petrified in the dark.

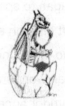

Chapter 30

'A Hard Nut to Crack'

An elderly gentleman in a dark uniform with gold braid stood at the main doors of the museum. He looked at his watch as he liked to be punctual for his late shift. He had just locked the doors after the curator and the rest of the museum staff had left. He did not really like the night shift as it was lonely and boring with no one to speak to and nothing ever happening. In fact the best shift was the early morning one when the cleaners were in. They always talked to him and had a good laugh while they worked, playing pranks on one another. He checked his torch and started his rounds, which was the most exciting part of the night.

In the Large Mammals section of the museum Angus crept steadily along the passageway. He watched the shadows for any movement as he tried to keep his breathing steady and calm. Suddenly a shape loomed out from the shadows and he began to sprint for all he was worth towards the exit. He turned left through a doorway and caught a glimpse of the larger of the two men running after him. Angus tried to recall his name and then wondered why it mattered at a time like this. The next corridor appeared just after the Spiders section and he turned right towards the main entrance hall. He hoped the man could keep up and sneaked a backward glance to see where he was and that is when he hit the marble floor.

At least twenty minutes had passed without any sign of Angus or the men that chased them. Georgina was getting agitated and decided that she had to risk taking a look around. The frightened girl took a deep breath and stood up as she moved out from her hiding place. She tentatively walked along the corridor as shadow after shadow became more and more menacing and then relief once she realised it was just another model. Eventually she found the main entrance hall and saw Angus surrounded by their pursuers.

The darkness spun around him and then strangely blurred faces appeared in front of his eyes. He tried to sit up but the pain in his head seared through his brain.

"Get him up!" sniped a voice in the darkness.

"You might have killed him on that floor Miss… He took a hefty blow to the head after you tripped him" said the large man called Ron.

"That maybe so, but he has been very troublesome and at this point in time I do not care!" she growled.

Both the men helped Angus to his feet and the

young protector stood unsteadily and faced Meredith Quinton-Jones.

They were in front of the steps to the upper landing and moonlight streamed in through the glass windows in the roof. He looked past Meredith at the giant dinosaur skeleton that met visitors as they walked in through the main entrance and he fervently wished it would come to life and eat Meredith. His head hurt but he was going to see this through.

"So you thought you could hide in here hoping I would be too afraid to follow... well it would appear you were wrong!" spat the dark haired woman standing before him.

Angus did not answer, and instead rubbed the front of his head where a large bump was beginning to appear.

"Painful is it?" sneered Meredith. "Things are going to get a lot worse if you do not give me the eggs."

Angus looked her in the eyes defiantly and remained silent.

"What's in the bag Angus?" she asked.

"Nothing!" he replied taking a step back in a protective gesture.

"Take it from him and check it" she said to her men.

The man called Jeff tried to grab the bag and Angus fought to stop him getting it. They lad struggled valiantly against the stronger man and managed to pull away from him.

"Grab him Ron!" shouted the smaller man.

The large man grabbed Angus by the scruff of the neck using just one hand, and lifted him up off the ground. Angus swung his arms trying to hit the large man with his fists in an attempt to spring free from his grip, but it was all in vain and the back pack was forcibly removed from him. Jeff unzipped the bag and took a look inside.

"Are they in there?" asked Meredith not taking her eyes off Angus.

"Yes Miss they are" replied Jeff smiling up at her.

"Well Angus it looks like I win in the end… I will leave you to explain to the authorities after we've broken out of here" she smiled in triumph.

Georgina watched from behind one of the massive pillars in the hallway, terrified that Angus would be hurt in some way.

"Bring the bag and let's go" snarled Meredith to the men.

Ron dropped Angus onto the floor and as they began to walk away, the lad jumped to his feet and tried to retrieve the backpack. Meredith turned and grabbed Angus by the shoulders.

"Give it up, you've lost!" she screamed into his face and then pushed him backwards onto the floor.

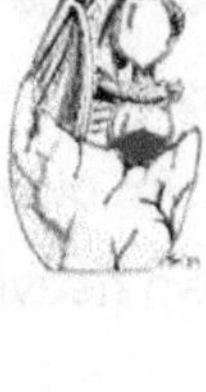

Angus' head spun with the pain from his bump and he knew he had done enough so he jumped up and ran back the way he had come.

"Leave him! We have what we want" said Meredith to Ron as he started to give chase.

The trio turned towards the exit doors of the museum and in Georgina's direction, so she left as silently and as quickly as she could back to the dinosaur section.

By the time Georgina reached the hiding place, Angus arrived at her side panting heavily. They jumped behind the screen and Angus rubbed his head as the pain throbbed through his temple.

"Did they hurt you?" she asked, concerned.

"A little bump on the head, that's all, but they took the bait and it was worth it" he replied smiling.

"Let me see…" said Georgina, "Angus that is really bad! You could have concussion; we need to get you to hospital!"

"I'm fine…" he began, and then stopped when he heard someone in the passageway.

Both of the protectors looked out apprehensively to see who was there.

An old man walked slowly up the passageway and sat down heavily in a chair marked 'NHM staff only', only feet from

the model nest. It was warm in the Museum because the radiators were on full heat to keep the visitors comfortable during the winter months. The warmth made Archie Power feel sleepy and he usually had forty winks around this time of his shift, after his rounds. It was all right for the visitors as they left their winter coats in the museum's cloakroom so they could enjoy their wanderings through the exhibits. He loosened his collar and took out his evening newspaper and glanced at the sports section to see whom his football team was playing that weekend. A London derby no less and by all accounts it would be a cracker! Satisfied of his team's chances of winning he refolded his paper, tucked it down the side of the chair and folded his arms across his chest to have a little snooze.
Georgina stared at the dinosaur nest from behind the scenery and could scarcely believe it when she saw one of the eggs move. She nudged Angus and his eyes opened wide when he saw what was happening. The two protectors were not the only ones to notice as Archie watched one of the dinosaur eggs move slightly. The eggs were hatching early!

"Now Archie my son don't get worked up but I think you might be dreaming" said the old man to no one in particular, leaning forward in his chair for a closer look.

A tiny crack appeared on the top of the egg and Archie slowly stood and walked to the rail to have a closer look. The crack got bigger and bigger until a tiny head with blinking eyes poked out of the shell. Angus desperately wanted to reach out and grab the eggs, but they could not risk being caught so he waited to see what the old man would do. Aches and pains now forgotten the old man jumped up and ran off in the direction of the main entrance.

Angus watched him disappear and then speedily vaulted the barrier and tucked the newly hatched dragon and the other egg inside his jacket. He had only just slipped back into his hiding place when the alarm sounded in the building, echoing throughout the corridors.

At the front exit, Meredith Quinton-Jones and her men had sized up the doors and she made contact with her other men as they waited outside the building in a van. The helicopter had been sent back after dropping them at an empty park just a few streets from the museum. Fortunately not many people had seen them land and it appeared that the Police would be none the wiser. They had the bag, now all they had to do was get out of the building.

"Well, can you open it?" she asked impatiently.

"Of course Miss. Just give me a couple of minutes" replied

Jeff as he bent to work on the lock.
He had barely begun when an old man came running up from the dinosaur section. The museum guard stopped dead in his tracks when he saw three people at the doorway. Without hesitation and before Meredith or her men could do anything, he ran to the nearest alarm and pulled the lever down. The sirens inside the building wailed as Jeff and Ron put their boots to the doors in an effort to speed up their exit. The men on the outside performed a similar action in an attempt to break the doors open. Archie, weighing up the situation, decided that discretion was the better part of valour and locked himself in a nearby office.

The heavy doors gave way under the double onslaught of Meredith's men and wasting no time they raced to the van parked at the roadside. Meredith grabbed the door and pulled it shut behind her.

"Get me out of here now!" she barked at the driver.
The man did not need telling twice and had already started to pull away from the building. He worked the clutch and accelerator in quick succession as he raced through the gears and pushed the van up to top speed. They managed to get to the end of the building when a police car careered around the

corner and crashed into them. Before they knew it, Meredith and her men were surrounded by police cars and held captive whilst the police tried to get establish what on earth was going on.

Chapter 31

'Archie's Moment'

Angus and Georgina waited a few minutes until the alarm stopped and then decided they would venture out for a look. No one was in sight and they made their way cautiously down the passage towards the entrance hallway with the broken doors.

"Now's our chance… Let's get out of here!" said Angus holding one arm under his jacket to cradle the eggs close to his chest.

He could feel the movement of the hatching Fire Whelps and hoped that the baby dragons did not live up to there name.

Both of them tiptoed along the marble floor to the smashed exit doors until they could see outside. Angus stopped abruptly when he spotted the two policemen standing guard outside on the steps.

"We'll never get past them. What will we do now?" whispered Georgina in his ear, in a panic.

It looked pretty hopeless and they would get caught for sure as soon as they even tried to step outside the doors.

"We can't risk them finding the Fire Whelps…" replied Angus, "I guess we could always hide inside until morning."

It was a hopeful suggestion and one that may have been reasonable if it had not been for the hatching eggs. It really did not look good at all for them!

"Perhaps I can be of assistance?" said Pyrra behind him. The protectors turned to see her head and neck stretched inside the broken doorway leaving her body outside. The two policemen were none the wiser, as they could not see the invisible green dragon standing between them and the museum entrance. If she was invisible that meant the protectors were now invisible in her presence and both rushed forward to give her friendly face a hug.

"I take it you're pleased to see me, but I noticed Meredith has the backpack. Are you both okay?" asked Pyrra looking serious.

"Absolutely… and these two little whelps are keen to meet their mum!" said Angus as he opened his jacket slightly. The green dragon's eyes lit up when she saw that both of the dragon eggs had already hatched and she smiled broadly at both protectors.

"I would be greatly interested to hear how you managed this trick Angus, but that will have to wait until we get you out of here" she said.

Both of the protectors gratefully jumped up onto her back and gently and very quietly she slipped passed the two policemen and rejoined Wymarc on the roof of the building.

The police, having managed to find poor Archie and coax him from his hiding place, brought him to the scene of the crash. The cowering security guard immediately identified the people in the van as the intruders from inside the museum. Now Meredith had a lot of explaining to do; especially when the police searched the car and found two stolen dinosaur eggs. Archie spotted them and immediately claimed they belonged to the museum. The director of the museum arrived looking greatly upset at the damage and got even more distressed when he saw the two eggs in police custody.

"But why would they steal these worthless imitations?" he asked confused.

"Begging your pardon Sir, but them eggs is real and what's more I saw one of 'em hatch in the museum!" said Archie proudly.

The policemen nearby stood staring open mouthed at the security guard. The director looked sympathetically at the old man as it had obviously been a traumatic night for him. Meredith had a look of absolute horror on her face.

"What do you mean you saw one hatch? Where exactly did

you see this?" she demanded imperially.

She had asked the question with such authority it did not enter into anyone's head that she had just been caught in the act of breaking into the museum.

"In the dinosaur section Miss" replied the old guard truthfully.

Meredith touched a ring on her left hand that was glowing slightly and started to look around as if searching for something, her eyes wild.

"Where are they?" she shouted to no one in particular as she scanned the Natural History Museum's facade.

When Meredith and her party were arrested, the police had searched them all and removed whatever they had on them. The policeman that gathered it all together was amused by this crazed woman's antics. He studied the items that had been taken from the men and apart from the usual things like the lock picks, all the men carried strange blue stones. He held them in his hand now.

"Look up there!" shouted Meredith. "They're the ones you should be arresting!"

Everyone turned to look up at the roof of the building.

Pyrra, Wymarc and the two protectors stood on the roof and watched the proceedings below. Meredith's men had been handcuffed and placed inside the police van. The flashing blue lights lit-up the buildings eerily as a crowd gathered nearby to watch the spectacle. Angus watched Meredith and the museum guard, speaking in an animated fashion in the middle of the street. Then he saw Meredith scanning the building as if looking for something. She had just pointed in their direction when Angus told them all to hide.

Everyone in the street that heard her shout looked in the direction she was pointing, including PC Rob Brighton who had the Dragonore taken from Meredith's men, in his hands at the very moment he looked up. The Curator and the police sergeant looked at each other then at the woman before them.

"There's no-one up there Madam" said the Sergeant looking her straight in the eye.

"But they were there I tell you… send your men up at once!" she screamed hysterically looking from one unsympathetic face to another.

Then she spotted the white face of PC Brighton and she recognised that look. It was the look of someone who had just seen myth and legend come to life before their very eyes.

Now PC Brighton was a simple copper and his usual daytime shifts tended to follow the same sort of pattern; giving directions to tourists; being photographed with them; teaching road safety lessons in schools and directing the traffic; but none of his training had prepared him for this!

"He's seen them!" screamed Meredith, "Go on ask him! Tell them what you can see!"

All eyes now turned to the poor constable as he stood with four stones in his hand.

"Well Rob did you see anything up there?" asked the sergeant.

Police Constable Rob Brighton weighed up his career in one swift moment and answered.

"No sir… nothing at all and as you can see sir there's nothing on the roof" his face deadpan.

The fact was, thanks to the Dragonore he had confiscated, he had seen two young teenagers and what looked like a blue and a green dragon watching the street from the roof. They disappeared as soon as he saw them, but they were there, and he was never going to admit it to anyone, ever!

Meredith on the other hand was very aware of the dragon's presence on the roof because she still had her Dragonore. She had a ring made with the precious gem set in it and she watched it glowing gently on her finger.

"They're up there and if you take one of those stones you'll be able to see the dragons!" she shouted.

The silence that followed was deafening as every eye watched Meredith as she stood and pointed at the stones in PC Brighton's hand. The sergeant had heard enough from the crazy woman and took charge of the situation.

"PC Brighton, take those things away... You two grab her and put her in the van with the others and I'll call the police psychiatrist to meet us at the station!"

Angus sneaked a look from behind one of the animal statues on the roof and witnessed Meredith being led away by two officers. She looked back at the roof and caught Angus' eye, shooting him a look that suggested this was not finished.

The director walked back to survey the damage to his museum and turned to dear old Archie Power.

"Now tell me again about these eggs Archie?" he said kindly.

The old guard loved his job and he removed his glasses and rubbed his eyes. He could have sworn blind that he had just seen a dinosaur hatch, but of course no one would believe him; and having just witnessed what had happened to Meredith, he decided to use his powers of self preservation once again.

"I think I might have been mistaken sir... probably all the excitement" he replied carefully.

"I thought that might be the case" smiled the head curator,

"and I'm not surprised! We owe you a debt of gratitude Archie… you're a hero!"

"I am?" Archie grinned at the curator

As they talked about a special reward from the museum he thought about getting home. He was looking forward to a cup of tea and perhaps a chocolate biscuit. Maybe he could tell his wife Maud all about it later. She would believe him!

Chapter 32

'Fools Errand'

One week later two dragons carried their protectors over the Irish Sea on a very familiar journey to Calmor. They entered the hidden cavern below the castle and flew up the main passage that led from the secret entrance. Both protectors jumped down from the dragons and shook the rain water from their jackets. Two baby dragons played together as they tumbled about in the middle of the cavern floor. One had just started to show hints of turning red and the other was still a neutral brown. Pyrra had explained to Angus that all dragons are born that way and only got their colouring after a few weeks. The lad watched the Fire Whelps playing and smiled when they stopped and looked in his direction. As soon as they recognised him, both of them scurried as quickly as they could in his direction and jumped on him. He fell backwards with one of them licking his face and the other pulling at the sleeve of his jacket.

"Now you two, leave Angus be for a second and let him get his coat off!" said Rhys.

The red dragon had been reunited with her babies at Calmor and the thanks and bravery speeches that followed, had embarrassed Angus as usual. The lad loved both Aedan and Ceamantya, but he was particularly fond of Aedan who had hatched first and probably thought Angus was a bit like a father. Their real father, Swithin was extremely proud and very grateful indeed to the four of them for retrieving the eggs. Rhys promised as soon as the baby dragons could fly and were strong enough they would go to London to thank the City Guardians personally. Before that they would have to be taken to Krubera to get the precious Heart Stone and that was something Angus looked forward to seeing. They already had news that Faris had made a swift recovery from his ordeal and that all the City Guardians were fit and well. Rathlin had visited them several times since the return of the eggs and the dragons were very happy to be part of the growing family that was the Secret Society of Dragon Protectors.

"Have you seen the newspapers recently?" asked Rathlin handing a newspaper to Angus.

The lad looked at the headline on the front page and there was a small paragraph about a woman being prosecuted for breaking into the Natural History Museum of London. The article described the female head of a well respected company that had apparently had an episode of some sort. Angus thought it was just as well they did not have the rest of the story!

The others had moved on and only Rathlin remained

"So Pyrra has told me some strange things happened to you at Halcyon House" he said.

"She did?" asked Angus, acting surprised by the comment.

"She did indeed, and I think we need to discuss them with Godroi and Finian in the very near future" replied the leader of the SSDP. Rathlin saw the worried look on the lads face. "But enough of that… let's join the others and celebrate with some of Dermot's flapjacks!" clapping Angus on the back.

They strolled away, talking amiably about the latest events in the SSDP and completely unaware of another event some 5000 miles away.

An old man sat by his simple home in a small province in China. His great grandson stood nearby as the old man tried to convince him of something whilst speaking Cantonese.

"Great grandfather I've told you before, I want to speak in English! All the kids in school are using English these days" said the boy impatiently.

The old man looked at his great grandson and shook his head.

"You must not turn your back on the ancient ways Yingjie" replied the old man in English.

"That's all you talk about great grandfather, but the old

ways are not going to do me any good in the modern world" said the young teenager.

"You would be surprised!" said the old man smiling wisely.

"Sorry, but I need to go and meet my friends. I'll see you later at dinner" replied Yingjie and with a weak smile he turned and left.

The old man watched the boy walk off towards the town centre and he shook his head disappointedly and sighed as he began to pack some loose tobacco in his long pipe. His home was located in a dense bamboo forest on the side of a mountain. The bamboo trees were very thickly grouped together and the

shadowy darkness of the forest pressed in around the small clearing. The old man's long white hair and beard lay on his simple blue tunic and he began to puff thoughtfully on the pipe.

"You can come out now!" called the old man.

At first nothing happened, but then the strong bamboo trees parted easily as the darkness beyond began to expand. A black dragon stepped into the sunlight, his red eyes fixed on the old man as he casually smoked his pipe.

"You took your time old man… I was beginning to think you would never sense my presence!" snarled the dragon.

"I was busy with my great grandson" replied the old man casually as he sent a perfect smoke ring into the air. "What do you want?"

"Ah straight to business, I like that… I want the object!" smiled Felspar.

The old man seemed unconcerned by this strange request.

"And what object would that be?" asked You Longwei innocently.

Felspar looked down at the ground and used his right fore claw to paw at the earth.

"You would be wise not to waste my time old man!" growled the dragon. "Now I will ask you one more time, where is it?"

"I can assure you I will never tell you where it is and you will never make me tell you!" replied the old man coolly.

The strike was so fast that You Longwei could never have seen it coming. Nonetheless, the old man was not in his chair when it disintegrated into small splinters; smashed by the dragon's tail. The old man had morphed into a dragon carving on the roof of his home.

"I'm impressed old man. I didn't know humans could do that, but it won't save you. I know how to get you back out again!" the dragon sneered.

The old man did not reply as Felspar lifted his tail again, the sharp point of the tail aimed at the statue.

"I cannot kill you whilst you're in there, but I can certainly destroy your hiding place!"

His tail slashed down on the wooden carving and sliced it in two. The old man's human shape morphed out of the carving and landed haphazardly on the ground. Felspar grabbed him up by one leg and lifted the old man upside down dangling him in front of his black snout.

"Now this can be done the easy way, or you can find out how if feels to be eaten, one piece at a time, by a dragon!" snarled Felspar into the man's face. "Oh, and if you're really lucky, I might even cook you first."

The dragon inhaled deeply then narrowed his red eyes and stared intently into Longwei's.

"Now let's try again… where is it?"

Mosman

'The City Guardians'

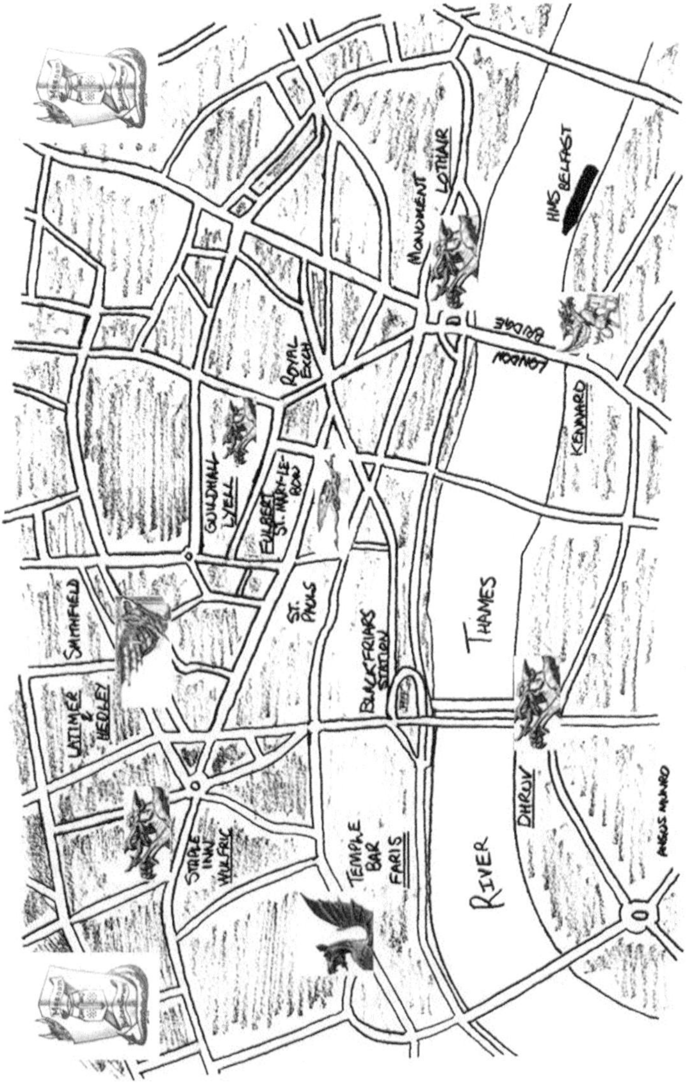

Three years ago when Debi and John first discussed ideas for 'The Dragon's Tale', neither of them could have possibly imagined what they were taking on. The excitement of releasing a book is tremendous, however one that you have solely produced and published brings an intensity of feeling that is beyond words, but perhaps best described as bringing a child into the world. You have all the trepidation and worry of a new parent, but add to that the stress of wondering how your best efforts will be received. Indeed the world of the SSDP has now grown so much that each book becomes more intricate. This is not so much due to the complexity of the storyline, but more so, the responsibility of ensuring that the history and rules created in previous books, are maintained throughout as accurately as possible. John especially has a newfound appreciation of his own literary hero; Sir Terry Pratchett and is extremely proud of producing four books in three years!

Look out for book six in the series.

The Secret Society of Dragon Protectors

Due for release in 2013!

For further details or to become a member of the SSDP visit the official website at

www.thesecretsocietyofdragonprotectors.com